D1255420

The Little Red Phone

By Henry Kane

THE TRIPOLI DOCUMENTS
LUST OF POWER
A KIND OF RAPE
DECISION
THE MOONLIGHTER

THE
Little

Red Phone

by Henry Kane

ARBOR HOUSE
New York

Library of Congress Catalogue Card Number: 81–71669

ISBN: 0–87795–375–9

Manufactured in the United States of America

10   9   8   7   6   5   4   3   2   1

To Florence and Hank Bernstein,

dear friends and good soldiers
who stood up straight and true.

Be sober, be vigilant; because your adversary the devil, as a roaring lion, walketh about, seeking whom he may devour.

1 PETER 5:8

One ~∞∞~

ON THIS rainy day in April, a dark Saturday in New York City, Maureen Blair, in a corner of the cab, wished forlornly for a cigarette. She had stopped smoking, it was almost a year, and would never return to smoking, but there were moments—of stress, and sometimes moments of nothing at all—when she experienced a pang, an anxious emptiness that with certain persons must perforce be forever: the lingering always-aftermath of addiction. She shook it off, smiled dourly; this day she was entitled. Stress. She was on her way to a session with a psychiatrist. First time.

She squirmed in her corner of the taxicab, admitting it was not in fact an occasion for stress because the psychiatrist, Dr. Samuel Vaughn, was a dear friend, and she was not on her way to a session because she would not be a paying client, she would be a friend visiting with a friend—except that the purpose of the visit was not social.

Stop it, she thought.

The sound of the ceaseless rain surrounded her.

Stop fighting yourself, she thought, stop trying to establish a rationale. You are on your way to a session with a psychiatrist, and it's about time—and again she fought herself. About time? And defended herself: delay had not been on *her* account. She had procrastinated, and kept procrastinating, because of Steven; to confide her problem would be terribly to embarrass Steven. But now it was necessary *because* of Steven (his very sanity) to seek out professional advice, and who better than Dr. Sam.

They had been friends all their adult lives, Sam Vaughn and Steve Blair: so who better than Dr. Sam? She had made the call from the outside, not from home, and doc had responded quickly and cheerfully; she had called him Thursday afternoon and he had set the appointment for Saturday at four. "You won't be pressed, you'll have all the time you want," he said. "I'm entirely free after four o'clock."

Samuel Vaughn's office was in a high rise on Fifty-third Street, east of Fifth Avenue. The office—waiting room and consultation room—was the first two rooms of an eight-room apartment in which Dr. Sam lived alone; he was long divorced from his wife. There was a canopy extending to the curb, and Maureen Blair, quitting the cab, ran under it; in the lobby she entered one of three elevators. She pushed for sixteen and on the sixteenth floor she walked the corridor to 16-A and touched the button. Dr. Samuel Vaughn himself opened the door.

"Hi, doc," she said. His closest friends, like Maureen and Steve, called him doc as though that were his Christian name. More formally to his friends, or for identification to friends, he was Dr. Sam. He took her hand and drew her in.

"Dear Maureen, hello," he said. "Stinking weather."

" 'April is the cruellest month.' "

"T.S. Eliot."

"You bet."

He took her umbrella, immersed it into an umbrella stand. She pulled off her rainhat, shook out her hair. He hung away her raincoat, returned to her and smiled. "Beautiful as ever," he said.

"Thank you," she said easily, perfunctorily. It was a compliment she had heard all her life.

She moved toward the tall pier mirror he was wise enough to have on a wall of the waiting room. She took a comb from her purse and fixed her hair, ash blond; once long ago that term had been platinum blond. She was in truth a redhead, but she had dyed her hair blond because of the kids and because Steve had black eyes and black hair. It obviated the many questions that had been asked at the beginning; the kids had white blond hair and light blue eyes.

She had blue eyes. And a small nose, a good chin, a good jaw. She was tall with a willowy figure that was spoiled—at least in her opinion—by breasts that were too large. She was thirty-two and looked younger.

"This way," Vaughn said, waving a cupped hand across his paunch of a stomach, gracefully.

She preceded him into the consultation room, large and square, with closed windows, but cool and airy because of the vents high in the walls. He indicated a chair and she sank into it. He went behind a huge mahogany desk and into a high-backed mahogany swivel chair. He sat there looking at her; then he was up and out of the chair, pacing, marching about the room on short sturdy legs; he ended his march at a window. He stood there, his back to her, his hands clasped behind him.

She understood and wordlessly thanked him. He was giving her time, giving her silence, letting her breathe. Dear God, he was so old, standing there by the window; small, round, pudgy; his white hair was a garland encircling a bald pink pate. She knew his age, fifty-three; he was only three years older than Steven Blair, but, dear God, he looked fifteen years older. Was it his work, his profession, this awful business of continually listening to people's sufferings? Or was it, just as likely, a matter of genes?

He turned. He said, "Would you like a little wine, a bit of white wine?"

She heard herself giggle. "Is that the way it goes, these permissive days? Psychiatrists serve wine to the patients?"

"Not at all," he said, "but you're not a patient." His deep slow voice was comfortable, comforting; a vibrant voice, resonant, a baritone. "And from the look of you, you're still locked. Do you think a bit of wine might help?"

"Yes."

"Won't be a minute."

He went out a door in the rear; came back carrying a tray with two long-stemmed glasses of wine. He put down the tray on his desk, took one of the glasses to a marbled-topped end table beside her chair. "Chablis," he said. He returned to his desk and sat in the swivel chair. He raised his glass. "Skoal," he said.

She sipped wine. She longed for a cigarette.

He said, "How're those beautiful kids of yours?"

"They're fine, beautiful, just great." And then immediately she was angry. Good old Dr. Sam, she thought, doing a number on me, trying to get me over the hump with the usual silly rote questions. And I fell right into it, first question, with the usual silly rote reply. Dear Dr. Sam, I did not come here to talk about the kids, or anyone, or anything, except Steven Blair. She sat forward. She said, "He's sick; I think he's sick . . ."

"I know."

"He's become tight, irritable, terribly withdrawn." She cocked her head; squinted at the man behind the desk. "You know? Did you say you *know*? How the devil . . . ?"

"He told me."

"Steve?"

"He came here."

"When?"

"Couple of weeks ago. Actually, to preempt you. He was certain you were about to be in touch with me. He knew—felt in his bones—that you were getting ready. He wanted to be on his own case, before *you* got on his case."

"So, doctor, what was your diagnosis?"

"Depression."

"What in the old days my mother would have called a nervous breakdown?"

"Yes."

"And my grandmother would have called creeping melancholia?"

"Precisely."

"What do we do about it, Dr. Sam?"

He sipped the wine. "If you wouldn't have called me, I'd have called you."

"So what do we do about it, Dr. Sam?"

"He needs therapy."

"But he won't go for therapy—or didn't he tell you?"

"He told me." Vaughn had a round, florid face, and little eyes deeply wedged in sockets of fat. "We can't perform therapy like, for instance, an emergency appendectomy." The little eyes looked sad. "If a nonpsychotic refuses therapy, it cannot be compelled."

"He's not psychotic."

"Of course not."

"So what do we do?"

Vaughn finished his wine. "A short lecture," he said and smiled. "First and foremost there must be, on our part, simpatico. Steve is at that witching age—fifty. A couple of years before fifty, or a couple of years after, the male of our species is at his own climacteric." He propped his elbows on the desk, enclasped the fingers of his hands. "The climacteric in the male is roughly the equivalent of the menopause in the female. Although usually there's no diminution of sexual activity, there is always more or less—the more or the less depending on the individual—an emotional upheaval that, in certain types, can touch on a mental health problem."

"There has been diminution."

Vaughn unclasped his fingers. "The term in common usage today—depression. As you said, in your mother's time it was called nervous breakdown and in your grandma's time it was melancholia—but in all times a man like Steve would be a likely candidate."

"Why?"

"A matter of temperament. People like Steve—sensitive, serious and, in a manner of speaking, inclined toward pessimism—they're almost sure-fire prospects for mid-life depression. But therapy in these cases—even short-term therapy—is likely to be quite helpful."

"Except he refuses to go for therapy."

"That's our problem."

"There's another problem."

"I've given him advice, however, and happily he's accepted it." Vaughn picked up his glass. It was empty. He put it down. "Which is why, dear Maureen, if you wouldn't have called me when you did, I'd have called you."

"For what?"

"Discuss Steve's problem; discuss the advice I gave him. None of it can happen without you."

"And what, please, is this advice that so happily he's accepted?" She did not like the sound of her voice; it betrayed rage. And for so long she had fought against that rage.

"Sabbatical," Vaughn said. "For the two of you. A year's sabbatical. You're overdue, both of you. You've neither had a full sabbatical. Go up there to the house in Maine; could do a world of good. Steve loves the beach, the ocean, the fishing, but it's always been a month or so in summer. You two have never done the winter thing, the snow, the winter recreation, a full year away from the *Sturm und Drang* . . ."

"Do you really believe that can help him?"

"There are various avenues of therapy. Before, you quoted T.S. Eliot. I've a quote for you, more pertinent. Dr. Karen Horney. 'Life itself still remains a very effective therapist.' "

Maureen drew a deep breath. "Did he talk sex with you?"

"What do you mean?"

"Impotence."

"No."

"We've not had sex . . . it's now eleven months and fourteen days. I know exactly: eleven months and fourteen days."

Samuel Vaughn opened a drawer of his desk, took out a pipe and a pouch of tobacco, filled the bowl of the pipe,

16

struck a match, puffed, blew smoke. "Now tell me, dear Maureen."

"I told you."

"Please tell me again."

"No sex. Impotent. Nor does he have desire. There's been . . . nothing. Eleven months, fourteen days."

"Jesus," Vaughn said, smoking his pipe. "And you a Roman Catholic."

"Jesus," Maureen said. "And what the hell is that supposed to mean?"

"Means you wouldn't be one to cheat."

"I'm not *that* Roman Catholic."

"Have you?"

"What?"

"Cheated?"

"No."

"See what I mean?"

"No sir, Dr. Sam, I do not see what you mean."

"How much Roman Catholic are you?"

"Not much anymore, I'm afraid. I was twenty-two when I married Steve; ten years now within the influence of a man eighteen years my senior. He is, as you know, an agnostic. Agnostic. Never had the nerve to say flat-out atheist. That's his way, isn't it? Never hits full strength, never swings for the home run, if you'll pardon the baseball metaphor. Steve Blair, always and for all time, the consummate bunter."

"Introvert. A shy man."

"Yes, that he is."

"But you knew it before you married him. You went with him for a year—you were lovers—*before* you married him. Why, now, the complaint?"

"Don't put words in my mouth, Dr. Sam. I'm not complaining. You asked about Roman Catholic, and I tried to answer. Influence of Steve, I've backed off from the church, I'm no longer a churchgoer. Nevertheless, I do believe, devoutly, in God Almighty. How about you?"

"I'm not ritualistic, no church, but I believe in God."

17

"Steve? What do you think?"

"He's the most honest man I know."

"So what?"

"He's a skeptic by nature. In religion he's never been shown, or convinced, that God exists. Therefore in his honesty, because of his honesty, he remains unconvinced. Why do you put him down for that?"

"Who's putting him down? Why, suddenly, are you my adversary, doc?"

He nodded. "Yes, you're right, I'm sorry. Unconscious. Involuntarily, I'm defending him. Because he is so vulnerable, if you know what I mean."

"I know exactly what you mean. I was trying to explain why Maureen Blair, once a dedicated Roman Catholic, is now a pretty lousy Roman Catholic."

"And I was trying to explain why you—no matter your problem—wouldn't be one to commit adultery."

"And I was trying to explain why you're wrong." Maureen tilted her glass and sipped at the dregs of Chablis. "I'm human. Like almost a year of celibacy; human. If I'd have met a man who interested me—really interested me—I'd have gone over. I don't deny my Roman Catholic training would have inhibited a lot of it—but, human. I mean I could go over, and no matter I had the hots for the guy, the poor bastard would have to have the patience of Job . . ."

Dr. Samuel Vaughn grinned. "How about me?"

"Never in your life."

"That's what I thought." He puffed his pipe. "Do you love him?"

"Steve?"

"Well, who else?"

She sat back in her chair.

He sat back in his chair.

They stared at one another, opaquely.

"Ten years," she said.

"I know the arithmetic," he said.

"Once, I was madly in love with him."

"Now?"

"You're the shrink, doctor. Ten years takes the shine off, doesn't it?"

"Yes, it does. It can. Do you love him?"

"Did you ask him if he loved me?"

Vaughn smoked his pipe. "Confidential," he said.

"I think he loves me and I think I love him—in what I would call the ten-year syndrome. I'm not mad about him anymore and I don't think he's mad about me. I'd say we're fond of each other and we *owe* each other. I would never let him down—no matter what—and I don't think he'd me— no matter what."

"Would you want to divorce him?"

"I don't think so—but mostly because of the kids. I think my best answer would be this: If he wanted a divorce, he'd have my consent . . ."

"He does *not* want a divorce, I can assure you."

Her eyes challenged him. "Is that good or bad, Dr. Sam?"

"In view of what you've told me—the impotence—I'd say good. If he doesn't believe the marriage is over, then he does believe the impotence is temporary—and I'm inclined to agree. Impotence is frequently a factor in depression."

"What do we do?" She felt the sting of tears at her eyes. "We no longer sleep in the same bed; point of fact, we now sleep in different rooms. Early on, I wanted him to come to you, he and I together. He refused. I realized . . . I mean . . . the embarrassment. So I suggested we go to a stranger, a specialist, a marriage counselor—he refused."

"Consistent, isn't he?"

"*What do we do?*"

"Do you want to leave him?"

"No."

"Then my best advice—the sabbatical. He's already begun to work it out at the school. A year up there on holiday in Maine, it might do it all; it's quite possible things will fall into place."

"I hate that house."

"No you don't. What you hate are the circumstances that gave you ownership of the house." He laid his pipe into an ashtray. "I repeat the quote from the estimable Dr. Karen Horney. 'Life itself still remains a very effective therapist.' Give it a chance. From what you've told me, you don't really have an alternative. And, quite possibly, it can work. Cause and effect. The effect of the depression is the impotence; thus, if the cause, the depression, becomes dissipated . . ."

Maureen stood up. "You're the doctor, doc."

"Please give it the full try." He went round to her, kissed her cheek. "It can work; I do believe it can work. Keep in touch with me. Tell him you've been here. And tell him I told you that he also was here—he does want you to know. At least like that, those decks will be cleared. But you keep in touch. I want to know how things are shaping up—good or bad. Promise me."

"I promise. And I thank you." She kissed him. "For everything."

She came home to an empty apartment. The rain had stopped but it still hung there in the sodden skies: it was dark outside. She switched on lights, put away the umbrella, took off raincoat and rainhat and went to the refrigerator. That was the point of communication in the Blair household; often there were many notes, attached by Scotch tape to the door of the refrigerator: reminders to herself, notes to the kids, notes from the kids, notes to Steve and vice versa. This time there was a single note.

> Maury: Josh is hungry, Laura is hungry and so am I, and they want to see the movie at the Waverly, and so do I. We're going out to eat and to the movie. See you later. Love, Steve.

She was glad. This once she was happy to be alone in the large apartment: six rooms in a high house on Sheridan Square at an awesome rental. She removed her clothes and went in for a shower, a cold dry martini on her mind. She came out, donned a lightweight kimono, went barefoot to the kitchen and began to make the martini. She was old-fashioned, she used gin rather than vodka, although she had recently read that gin was coming back into fashion. To hell with that. She was not one for fashions. Simply, she preferred gin in her martini: Beefeater gin, a smidgen of Cinzano dry vermouth, a dash of bitters, a great deal of ice and a vigorous stir with a long spoon. She strained it into a wine glass—there was too much for a cocktail glass—added a twist of lemon peel and went with it to the living room.

She sat with her martini and thought about Dr. Sam, Steve, the kids, the house she hated in the township of Acheron Falls in the state of Maine, and how it all began.

Two ~∞∞∞~

Maureen Kirby was the red-haired beauty of the town of Washburn, population 2011, in Bayfield County, Wisconsin. Maureen Kirby, bright beyond her years, was a high-school graduate at age fifteen. Maureen's dream all her life had been New York, New York, and she expressed the desire to go to college in New York City.

"Never!" Maureen's mother said. "That sinkhole, that New York City, never while *I'm* alive!"

But the sides were drawn. Maureen's doting father, a prosperous dairy farmer, was on her side; Maureen's mother, strict and prim, was on the other side. Maureen's mother lost the fight, and she never forgave her daughter.

Maureen went off to New York, to Columbia University. She lived, as per arrangement, with the family of her father's second cousin, the Quentin Duncans, good and righteous people, and she was in her junior year at Columbia when the news came of her father's sudden death and she knew she would never go home. He had bequeathed a bit of money to her—the bulk of the estate dutifully descending to his faithful wife—but Maureen Kirby's inheritance was sufficient to pay for the balance of her education and for her to leave the Duncans for a small apartment of her own.

She had taken her master's degree in education, when her money began to run out. She was seeking a job as a teacher, but it was a period when such jobs were scarce; therefore, no matter reluctantly, she applied for work with the Ford model agency. She had picked the best, the most famous, perhaps because she wanted to be turned down, but, despite her lack of experience, she had been promptly accepted. She was a good model, but not great, because she did not like it. She considered it demeaning, peddling her beauty, but it was a living and she needed the money—for rent, food, clothes—while continuing to submit resumes for the one job she wanted as her lifework: schoolteacher. But—as later on Steven Blair would say—every cloud has a plutonium lining. At the beginning, not yet aware of his deeply sardonic nature, she had thought he was turning a phrase, tossing a waggish fillip at the tired old aphorism about every cloud has a silver lining.

The silver lining to Maureen's brief modeling career was Nina Mercer—Nina of the great open heart—dear Nina who became her best friend, and who like a mother hen took Maureen under her protective wing. She was then almost at her majority, almost twenty-one; Nina was ten years older. Nina Mercer! The golden Nina of international renown, the fabulous, shining, blue-eyed blonde. . . .

Eleven years before, as Nina Kasson, she had come from Norway to make her fortune in America and she had succeeded. She was the top model of the agency. She was married to the dynamic Jack Mercer, commercial artist, illustrator and burgeoning cartoonist, and she was the mother of the most beautiful pair of twins in all this world, Josh and Laura Mercer, thirteen months old.

The Mercers had a marvelous apartment in the exclusive Dakota and Maureen visited often and became acquainted with Jack Mercer who told her about his friend Steven Blair, and told her he would introduce her to his friend Steve not only because Steve, like she, was unmarried, and not only because they were both very attractive people, but also because Steve was a longtime teacher in the New York City school system, and knew a lot of important people in the system, and, if interested, he had the know-how, the clout, and the contacts that could land her a job. Maureen declared she would be "fascinated" to meet Jack's friend, but when it happened her insouciance abruptly fell away: Steven Blair was totally unexpected.

At the time Maureen Kirby was introduced to Steven Blair, she had been living in New York City for upwards of five years. She had met many men described as "terribly" or "very" attractive and had learned, initially to her consternation, that they didn't live up to advance billing. She had learned that in New York City a man described as terribly attractive was a man with regular features who dressed well. She therefore had small hopes but great respect for the schoolteacher—grade-school teacher—she was about to meet. Nina said he was brilliant and Jack said he was *damn* brilliant, but Maureen knew he was a gentleman verging on middle age: he was a year older than Jack Mercer who was then thirty-eight.

When Steven Blair arrived that day at the Mercers' apartment, Maureen's first impulse was to curl up and die. She was wearing no makeup. Her hair was back in a severe ponytail. Her attire was what she had deemed proper for a meeting with a middle-aged schoolteacher: flat heels, a figure-hiding loose dark suit and a blouse with a chaste white Peter Pan collar. She took one long stupified look as Jack introduced them, and kept looking.

The son of a bitch was absolutely gorgeous.

Middle-aged? The guy was young and beautiful.

She was a moviegoer and a Gregory Peck fan, and this guy was her type. He had to be six two, but straight up, no round shoulders, an imperious carriage. He was dark; he had large, black, almond-shaped eyes; he had a high-bridged patrician nose; he had shiny, curly, jet black hair.

"Maureen Kirby," Jack Mercer said. "Steve Blair."

"I've heard so much about you, Miss Kirby. I've been looking forward . . ." Quiet, gentle, his voice was a dramatic contrast to the volatile buccaneer-type good looks.

"Yes," she mumbled. "I, too, been looking forward."

Thereafter it was drinks, a great many drinks, and small sandwiches and delicious conversation—with Steven Blair in the forefront and Maureen hanging back; the man blithely chatted of all manner of things, many of which she knew nothing about.

She was even then, in those first moments, almost in love.

He was unique. She had never met anyone like him. He was so romantically handsome she had to avert her eyes to keep from staring at him. But he was so much more, so much the intellectual, and so fluent in his wonderful command of the language. He was the hit of the party that day, he was the cynosure, the brilliant conversationalist who held them all in thrall.

And then the phone rang, it was Dr. Samuel Vaughn, and he came to the Dakota with his wife Loretta—he a chubby little man, she tall and thin; he a psychiatrist, she an anthropologist—and the young Maureen was entirely overwhelmed.

They went out to dinner; the talk was lively, some of it serious, some of it bantering, and they all talked except Maureen; and a lot of it, perhaps for her benefit, was about themselves. She did not talk because she was abashed in the presence of these others; to begin, she was ten years younger than the youngest, Nina, and she was twenty-one years younger than the eldest, Dr. Samuel Vaughn; she felt like a child in the company of adults, and a great deal of their conversation was in fact over her head. But she learned that the men were friends since boyhood, a triumvirate, the musketeers; and she also learned, to her amazement, that Samuel and Loretta, apparently a happily married couple, certainly a convivial couple, were right then in the midst of the legal procedures that would terminate their marriage.

Steven Blair took her home and she invited him in for a nightcap. Even then, so early on, she was devoted to martinis, and she offered the same to him but he shook it off in favor of a brandy—except there was no brandy in the house. (Thereafter, for the rest of her life, wherever she lived, there was always a bottle of brandy in the bar.)

They drank martinis.

He said, "I might be able to help you."

"Oh?" Querulously, the blue eyes blinked.

"To teach school."

"Oh!"

"Jack has filled me in on you, a good deal about you. I want you to know that Columbia's highly regarded in this town, and a master's—"

"So how come I can't get to first base?"

He sipped his martini. "It's a bad time. These days they're firing teachers rather than hiring them. However, if one knows the ropes . . ."

"Do you know the ropes, Mr. Blair?"

"Steve."

"Steve. *Do* you know the ropes?"

"Yes."

They had a stretch of silence. He drank his martini, she drank of hers, and wondered about him. Grade-school teacher. In New York City it was called elementary school. Steven Blair was an elementary-school teacher—he taught seventh grade—in a school in Greenwich Village. But Jack Mercer had told her that Steven Blair had top honors, that the guy was a Ph.D. Jack Mercer had told her that Blair had acquired his doctorate while teaching in the elementary school in Greenwich Village.

"Why?" she said.

"Why what?"

"Jack Mercer's also filled me in on you. Ph.D. It doesn't quite fit. I mean Dr. Steven Blair teaching elementary school, like seventh grade, y'know? Maybe the principal of an elementary school. Certainly a teacher in high school. Most properly, a college professor. But what in all heck in seventh grade in elementary school in Greenwich Village?"

The black eyes filmed over, then came back. "We do, or

26

try to do, all of us, what we want to do, don't you think, Miss Kirby?"

"Maureen."

"Don't you think, Maureen?"

"What we want to do? Yes, of course."

"Then let's leave it at that."

"I'm sorry," she said.

"We were talking about you. Your career—not as a model."

"Yes," she said eagerly.

"You're young, and, as corollary, naive. The world we live in, Miss Kirby—Maureen—is corrupt, venal, I'd say a sinkhole."

"Sinkhole." The martini was having effect: she chortled. "It's a word my mother used to use. Sinkhole. That's what she called New York City—a sinkhole."

"Your mother was correct, but she was looking from the wrong end of the telescope and she saw, narrowly, New York. Looking from the other end she would have seen it all, the whole world—a sinkhole." He smiled. "But for now let's concern ourselves with your mother's sinkhole. You want a job, you're qualified and I think I have the strings that can pull it off, put you to work, civil service and all, in my school in the Village."

"Please—will you do it?"

"I will try." But the soft voice was tentative.

Was that his way, his manner: tentative? Or, more plausibly in New York City the sinkhole, was he shyly putting out the proposition? I will do for you—if you will do for me. She was a virgin, but she was willing. Five years in New York City. For five long years she had been fighting off a lot of them, but now she was willing. Especially with this man.

She accepted his proposition. "Please try real hard," she said. Her tone of voice, the look in her eye, was unmistakenly an acceptance. She was open for him, wide open, but

27

he did not take her, and she knew it right then: he was a strange man. He drank his drink and stood up.

"Got to go. Got to be up early tomorrow."

"Sure," she said.

They went hand in hand to the door.

"It was lovely, Maureen."

"I loved it." She stood close to him and tilted her head; he ignored it. Still standing close she opened the door, slowly. He did not kiss her. "Good night," he said.

"Night, Steve."

She watched him going away, then closed the door and leaned against it. A strange man, she thought. Gay? Was that it? Was he gay?

Please God no, she thought.

She got the job. She taught fifth grade in his elementary school in Greenwich Village. They went out together regularly, often with Nina and Jack Mercer, and sometimes with Dr. Sam and whoever was his date for the evening. Months—and he did not kiss her, and she was ashamed—for his sake—to discuss it with the Mercers. Finally—and she had girded herself for days—she took the bull by the horns. "Are you gay?"

"No," he said.

"Don't you like me?"

"I love you."

"Then what is wrong?"

"I won't start what I can't finish."

"What the hell is that supposed to mean?"

They were in her apartment. He was drinking brandy—which now she always had in the house. She was drinking gin on ice with bitters. He said, "I know from Nina that you're a virgin."

"Am I supposed to be ashamed of that?"

"Of course not. But that's what I mean."

"What in hell *do* you mean?"

"What I said before . . . won't start what I can't finish."

28

"Where is it written that you can't finish?"

"Don't joust with me, Maureen."

"Who's jousting with you, Mr. Ph.D.?"

"Now look—you know my age. I'm old enough to be your father." He laughed. "I refuse to be a child molester. I refuse to take you to bed and seduce you."

"Now *you* look, Mr. Ph.D. Right now, this minute, I am going to take you to bed. And I am going to seduce you."

She gave up her apartment and moved in with him on Cornelia Street, walking distance from the school. She was happy; she had never been more happy in all her life.

"Never in all my life," she said to Nina Mercer.

"He's a wonderful man. Aside from my Jack, he's the most wonderful man in the whole damn world."

"So what the devil's wrong with him?"

"What do you mean—wrong with him?"

"You know darn well what I mean. Steven Blair, an absolutely brilliant man, and a brilliantly educated man. Ph.D. A doctor of philosophy teaching seventh grade in an elementary school? Something, somewhere, is very wrong."

"Not necessarily. There are people in this world without driving ambition. There are people who don't like to go out for the top rung—where they are vulnerable. There are people who are underachievers, because they feel safe where they are."

Maureen looked askance. "Is that the conclusion you've come to? You and Jack—is that the conclusion?"

"We think we know the reason."

"What?"

Nina was unhappy. "I'm sorry I opened my big fat mouth."

"What about?"

"Jack warned me. Sooner or later he said—because of what Maureen means to you—you are going to open your big fat mouth."

"Nina, darling, there's nothing sticky, nothing bad, you

29

can tell me about Steve Blair. I love the guy, remember?"

"Sterile."

"Oh, mother, are you wrong. Virile! My God, he never stops."

"Sterility has nothing to do with virility."

Maureen's eyes squeezed together. "You're so right. My marbles are rattling. Simply I'm dopey when the topic is Steve Blair."

"He ever tell you he was once married?"

"No! And why should he? I'm still new in his life, and as you damn well know, until he opens up, on any subject, he's a quiet man, deeply reserved."

"Well, hell, I'm telling, and to hell with Jack's warnings. I think it's good for you to know. I think it'll help you to understand a very intricate man. Married. He was twenty-one and the girl was twenty-one, and they were married for three years, and all along they wanted a baby, and nothing happened. Finally they went for tests. The girl was all right. Steve was sterile. They got divorced. But Jack believes—and I agree—it hit Steve hard. It hit where it hurts, in the *cojones*, the balls, the manhood, the *macho*, and that can be devastating to a young man. Jack believes it turned him inward, deprived him of the normal male-masculine drive for success; he considered himself a cripple and settled for the life of a cripple. He became a teacher in elementary school, and stayed there, safely. He continued his education all the way up to his doctorate, but that was for his own satisfaction, and not for any professional escalation. Why I'm telling you, Maureen, is because I wouldn't want you ever to try to push him. Where he is, and he's been there for all these years, he feels safe. If you push him, if he tries to get out of it, if he tries for up, he might fall out of kilter, and that wouldn't be good, it would not be good at all. Do you understand, Maureen? Do you understand why I'm telling you?"

"Yes. And I thank you."

30

They were married the next year. Maureen was twenty-two: Steven Blair was forty and filled with guilt. "It's lousy, it's no good," he said in his quiet voice. "The age gap is just too much. Now it looks pretty good, but, let's say in fifteen years, the husband will be an old cocker of fifty-five while the wife, comparatively, will be a youthful chicken of thirty-seven. Please remember, and never forget, that you're the one who's urging on us this legal connubial alliance."

"I want you for my husband."

"And I want you for my wife despite the fact that I realize, more than you, the enormous disparity in age, and despite the fact that I know, and now you know, that we cannot have children."

He had, of course, told her. He had told her about his early marriage, and the divorce, and the reason. "My sperm count is too low; my dearly beloved, you must accept the fact that no spawn, no offspring, hell, no children can result from this marriage."

She had railed at him then, making jokes skewering his first choice of word. "Spawn? The hell with spawn. Who cares? Spawn is for fishes." She was twenty-two and desperately in love and at that moment a throwback to Washburn, Wisconsin. She wanted to be legally wed to the man she loved, and to hell with spawn. Or offspring. Or progeny. Or whatever the hell word could be put up as an obstacle to the marriage.

The ceremony was performed in a small church on lower Fifth Avenue. The witnesses were Nina and Jack Mercer. The best man was Dr. Samuel Vaughn.

She was a happy bride and a deliriously happy wife, and the legal wedding and bedding seemed to have an effect even on such free souls as Jack and Nina Mercer. They became inseparable, the Mercers and the Blairs, uptown at the Dakota or downtown on Cornelia Street or around town at

31

plays, ballets, cabarets and, on occasion, on East Fifty-fifth Street at a lavish bash at the apartment of that convivial bachelor, the rotund Dr. Samuel Vaughn.

But best of all, for Maureen and Steve, was their relationship with the Mercer twins, the angelic Josh and the cherubic Laura, which relationship, whether or not the elder Mercers were aware, had radically improved after the Blairs' proper church wedding, and that improvement was the result of the new attitude of the free-wheeling Mercers toward their dear friends Steve and Maureen, now legally Mr. and Mrs. Blair. Now, often when Jack and Nina went away for a weekend, they left the kids with the Blairs on Cornelia Street. Or the Blairs went up and stayed with the kids at the Dakota. Or in the summer they would all go off for a vacation to Jack Mercer's house in Maine.

Maureen hated it.

She went because she loved the kids.

She hated that house even before the accident.

Jack Mercer, born in New York City, was an only child of elderly parents. He had a gift for drawing and his parents—indulging him in easel, canvas, oils and brushes—wanted him to be a painter. But Jack Mercer, even in early youth, was not one to delude himself; he realized he could never be a fine artist, but he also realized he could be a damn fine commercial artist, and from the beginning he pointed himself in that direction.

At age fourteen—a strong, rangy, stalwart blond with pale blue eyes—he had matriculated in Stuyvesant High School with an eye toward doing design drawing for advertising, and he had picked electives that could push him forward on that course. In one of those classes he had met Steven Blair, a sophomore and an editor on the high-school magazine, and Steve had dragged him to the office to meet the editor in chief, one Samuel Vaughn, then eighteen years of age (he had missed a year of school because of illness).

"This guy's out of this world," Steve Blair said to Sam

32

Vaughn. "We need him. I mean, give him a pen or pencil or whatever these people use, and he can draw you an illustration, or a straight portrait, or a crazy caricature, or whatever . . ."

It was then, in high school, that they fused to the triumvirate, the musketeers, a tight-close friendship that would continue for the rest of their lives. Sam Vaughn went on to NYU, and Steve followed and Jack followed Steve, but only Jack Mercer did not go on to graduate studies. Jack took a job with an advertising agency and was soon making a lot of money. And spending a lot of money. And then he met and married the exquisite Nina and they produced that gorgeous pair of twins.

"Gorgeous? Why the hell not?" said the hard-headed Jack Mercer. "Nina's the most beautiful blonde in the world, and I'm not half-bad, am I? So it figures for our kids. They figured to be gorgeous and they are. It's the bloodlines, baby. The good old chromosomes."

Nina laughed. "He's not as tough as he sounds," she said. "Inside he's a real softie."

He was tough *and* a softie. Tough: he refused a vice-presidency with his ad agency, because it entailed a lucrative but exclusive contract. He did not want to be tied down. He was doing free-lance illustrating for books and magazines. But what he enjoyed most was cartoons. He had the quick mind and facile pen to be a successful cartoonist, but the cartoon world was like a closed corporation, rough to break into: the market was small, the aspirants were many. But that was what he wanted, at end, as his career. Cartoonist. And he was beginning to nick at the edges; now and then, but not too often, one of his cartoons would hit with one of the big magazines.

Softie. Despite the lure of enormous fees, he refused to permit the twins to be models. "It's an unnatural life," he said. "It's got to hurt them in the psyche, if you know what I mean."

Nina agreed. "I know what you mean," she said.

33

Softie. Long ago, before Nina, he bought a home, sight unseen, in Maine, for his aging parents. His father, already ailing, was a transplanted New Englander, as was his mother, and they expressed the desire to die where they had been born; coincidentally they had both been born in the state of Maine, albeit his father in the north of the state, and his mother hundreds of miles to the south. "Sure," Jack Mercer said.

The old people knew what they wanted, and found what they wanted, and Jack bought it for them sight unseen because the price, perhaps expensive in Maine, was dirt cheap by New York standards. He was on his way to London then for six months of business manipulations—he was in fact already in London—when the deal in Maine was consummated. He had retained lawyers in Maine and they had cleared the title and he had cabled the money; he noted that the purchase price of a solid permanent house in the state of Maine totaled up to less than six months of business manipulations in the city of London.

His father had died in the house in Maine before Jack Mercer returned from London, and his mother had died up there that same year, but as Jack always insisted, it was not a house of death; it was also, very much, a house of birth. Because years later that's where the twins had been born, unexpectedly, prematurely, during a summer vacation; Jack himself, alone, had attended the delivery, and only after the twins were out of the womb and lying warmly on Nina's belly had he had the time to call the doctor.

But that was long ago.

Not really; not really long ago.

Four years. Only four years. Time flies, or holds still.

It was four years from the birth of the twins to the time of the accident.

Dr. Samuel Vaughn, like Maureen, but unlike Steve and Jack and Nina, was not crazy about the house in the township of Acheron Falls in the state of Maine. In point of fact it was not the house; it was the township of Acheron Falls, and quite possibly, it was the whole state of Maine. Dr. Sam was all big city, and most of all New York City.

"A rural area makes me nervous," he would say. "I swear to God, I get *lonely*. I swear to God I can't sleep at night because it's too damn *quiet*. You realize that silence can be awfully noisy, and that dead silence up there at Acheron Falls, it's virtually a cacophony."

He was not a hunter, a hiker, a jogger, a swimmer, and fishing—fishing most of all—bored him out of his head. On several occasions before and after the birth of the twins, and always in the month of August (because August is when psychiatrists take vacations), he had accepted—because he did not want to hurt the Mercers by constantly refusing—their invitation to come to Acheron Falls. He had stayed two days, three days—his record was five days—before packing up and rushing back to the heat and humidity of New York City.

Once, after just such a precipitate return, the good doctor and his good friends Maureen and Steve Blair were seated at dinner in the cool ambience of a fine, air-conditioned New York restaurant when Maureen—who then was still red-haired—grinned at him and crinkled her eyes. "At least in you I have an ally," she said. "You're the only other one who hates that house."

"Not really," Vaughn said. "The house is incidental. How can I say it?" He paused. "Simply, that rarified country atmosphere is not for me. I dislike that whole damn peaceful environment, admittedly beautiful. And since the house is right there in the middle of it, and in a sense the symbol of it, I dislike the house."

"Then we're not allies at all," Maureen said. "I love the town, I love the people—it's the house I hate."

"Why?"

"Because she's not playing with a full deck," Steve said. "I mean, on that subject, she's a little bit wacky in her beautiful belfry."

She waved him off. "The vibes," she said to Dr. Sam. "I get awfully bad vibes in that house."

"Nonsense," Steve said.

"I feel . . . like . . . it's a house of death."

Vaughn said, "Jack's parents died up there, in that house, within six months of each other. Do you think, perhaps, that's it?"

"I don't know. It's just . . . the best way I can express it . . . the vibes."

"Nonsense," Steve Blair said again. He did not believe in ghosts, specters, zombies, the undead, the occult, sorcery, spirit rappings and things that go bump in the night—and he did not believe in vibes. "Perfectly reasonable explanation," he said. "The locale. An isolation. Hell, a desolation. Next nearest house is eleven miles away. There it stands alone—stark, bleak, solitary—nothing close to it for miles and miles; that certainly can give it an aura of spookiness, especially to someone as impressionable, as sensitive as Maury . . ."

"He may be right, Maureen. As always, he sounds splendidly logical. What do you think?"

"It's quite possible he *is* right, but it doesn't do a thing for me. I can't change my insides, my guts: I still feel the same about that house. But, please . . ." She smiled. "Please don't mention any of this to Jack or Nina."

The accident happened eight years ago, when the children were four years old. Maureen blamed the house. She knew it was irrational; nevertheless it did offer a rationale, an excuse, some semblance of reason, albeit untenable, for her implacable hatred of the house.

Jack Mercer—with the kind of courage that made him so admirable to the quiet, temperate, unvaliant Steve Blair—had quit the advertising business and even the illustrating for the full go at free-lance cartooning; it had been a long and expensive struggle, but he was beginning to break through. He worked at home in the apartment at the Dakota but also, and somehow preferably, in the privacy of the remote house in Acheron Falls: the insular life was a prod to his creativity. Of course Nina would not let him stay alone in that big desolate house; always she and the kids accompanied him. It interfered with her career and her earnings dwindled—but his career was paramount.

Eight years ago. Early December. The Mercers had spent seven months in the house in Maine, seven productive months for Jack Mercer; now they packed and came home to stay the winter in New York. And they were home only a day when Jack discovered that he had failed to pack what was most important of all: the file that contained the cartoons that he intended proudly to display to the New York editors was still up there in Maine, locked in a drawer of his desk.

He laughed it off—leave it to Jack Mercer—and saw the good side of it. "Vacation," he said to Steve and Maureen. "Will you take care of the kids?"

"Of course," Maureen said.

"It's beautiful, just gorgeous weather," Jack said. "We'll drive up there alone, me and Nina—vacation. I'll pick up the file, and then we'll stay over for a few days, maybe a week, at one of those marvelous inns around Portland. Just me and my Nina. No kids. No work. And breakfast in bed. We'll go for the best. We'll eat and drink and be served like a king and queen, and loll around and live it up—vacation."

They left New York in the early morning of December nine. They were dead that afternoon. The car had blown a tire.

Jack Mercer's wallet gave the state troopers Steven Blair's name and address and the next day Steve was up there to identify, as best he could, the mangled bodies, and to arrange for the transportation home. "Never had a chance," a state trooper said. "He must've been goin' a pretty good clip. It's the front tire what blew, and that vehicle smashed up against a tree and wrapped itself around it. One thing I can tell you that's good—them two never knew what hit them. Them two poor folks passed without no pain, no suffering."

Maureen blamed the house. It was the house that had closed in on Jack Mercer's important file. It was the house that had demanded that Jack Mercer return to Maine. It was the house that had called them back—to their death—from New York City. It was the house, always that damned evil house—

"Now you *stop* it," Steven Blair said. "I *insist*, once and for all, that you stop this hoodoo-voodoo mumbo-jumbo. It's nonsense. It's damned arrant nonsense, and you damned well know it, and it's time you got off it."

The Mercers' reciprocal wills stated that the survivor was to be executor and sole heir. In the event that the Mercers were simultaneously deceased, their wills declared that Steven and Maureen Blair were to be coexecutors of the estate. In the event of such simultaneous decease, all of the Mercers' property, real and personal, was to be divided between their children, Joshua and Laura Mercer, except for the house in Acheron Falls, which was bequeathed in perpetuity to Steven and Maureen Blair. If at such time of testators' simultaneous decease the children were minors, then the coexecutors were to hold in trust all of Joshua and Laura's property until they came of age twenty-one, and at that time all such property would duly devolve . . .

The reciprocal wills were long and complex and filled with the usual tortuous legal language, but one clause stood out for the Blairs clear and imperative, and reasonable: "In the event of such simultaneous decease, and if at such time the above-named Joshua and Laura are not yet of legal age, then it is the request of the testators that their dearest friends, the said Steven and Maureen Blair, husband and wife, do apply to the courts for the purpose of legally adopting the said Joshua and Laura . . ."

"It's just pure damn lucky the kids have us," Steve Blair said and he was so right, always logical and practical. The children were only four years old; they did not yet understand the meaning, and finality, of death. They knew their mother and father were gone, but at once they had another mother and father whom they had always loved and who loved them. They were four; the transition was not difficult. It was much more difficult for Maureen, then twenty-four, and for Steve, then forty-two, and it was not because, as it turned out, the Mercers were less rich than the Blairs had presumed. "In fact we're dumb to be surprised," Steve said. "They were spenders, never stinted. They loved to live and they lived it up big, all the way."

The cooperative at the Dakota was heavily mortgaged; its sale produced no money for the estate. The Mercers' savings and investments totaled to $34,981.12. Jack's insurance policy showed a face value of $50,000; it brought $100,000, however, because his accidental death doubled the indemnity. Astonishingly, Nina had no insurance at all, but her safe-deposit vault contained $20,000 in cash. The legal fees—including the fee for the adoption proceedings—added up to $15,000.

The court ordered $10,000 immediately to be paid to the adoptive parents because of the need to expand their dwelling in order to include the children; the Blairs accepted because they could not have moved to proper quarters without it. The court also ordered that the Blairs could apply, from time to time, to withdraw monies from the trust estate for the ongoing support of the children. The estate was then in the net sum of $130,000—$65,000 for the care and education of each child—and the Blairs decided not to touch any of that money unless there was some urgent need.

They moved from Cornelia Street to the apartment on Sheridan Square. Maureen took a leave of absence; she felt that the children, deprived of their natural parents, should have their new mother—their adoptive mother—right there with them. At first the $10,000 that the court had awarded did help, but it quickly petered away; Steve's salary was insufficient to carry a family of four, and therefore in the evenings, with Steve home, Maureen went out to do private tutoring.

It was a struggle; but when the kids were old enough to go to school, it began to ease because Maureen was able to return to teaching. What with the inflation—and growing children—it continued to be a struggle. Which was the reason, during all these years, that Steve and Maury and Josh and Laura could only spend a month or so, every summer, up there at the house in Maine. The Blairs could not afford to have the full summer for themselves and for the kids: they had to teach summer school in New York City in order, of necessity, to augment their income.

But they never failed, for the sake of the kids, to work out at least a month every summer in the cool, salt-clean air of Acheron Falls by the sea in the state of Maine. And over the years her hatred of the house began to subside. "It's not really hatred, I don't think," she once said to Steve. "It's more, I dunno, a fear—some kind of weird, silly, irrational fear." But even that, the fear, with the passage of time, had begun to wane.

And now, of a sudden . . . sabbatical.

Doc had prescribed and Steve had accepted . . . sabbatical.

And Maureen Blair, at age thirty-two already set in her ways, was looking forward. Strangely, Maureen Blair, a creature of habit, was looking forward to the prospect of a full year away from all her accustomed habit patterns. Why? Why would a Maureen Blair want to go against the flow? Why would a Maureen Blair look forward to so drastic a turn-about in her life-style? The answer came slowly, it welled up from her loins: she was on her way to an adventure from which she would never escape. She knew, she was certain—the vibes—that she was on her way to a new life. Or to death. Or, however crazily, to both.

Life and death.

Death and life.

Oh God, dear Jesus.

Three ∿

THEY TOOK off on a glorious sun-drenched morning in June. They had spent weeks in preparation and days in packing; the Ford station wagon was heavily loaded.

Whatever had to be done, had been done. Steve was ill—in Dr. Sam's psychiatric language he was depressed—but at least until now he had lost none of his practical sense and none of his precise step-by-step methodology.

He had sublet the Sheridan Square apartment, payment in advance, for the full year, and at a good profit. He had done a full inventory and had packed everything additional they might need for the house in Maine—which was fully furnished and did contain all the basic appurtenances, including pots and pans and dishes and utensils. He had packed the many books he had bought over the years but were still unread because there was never time to read all he wanted; and he had not forgotten carefully to pack Josh's chemicals and lab equipment (chemistry was chief among the busy Josh's many hobbies).

He had put through a call to Maine, to Acheron Falls, for the utility company to turn on the gas and electric in the Blair house, formerly the Mercer house, and he had also called the telephone company. The gas and electric could be turned on by remote control; the telephones, however, could not be connected unless the house was open; there was tinkering to be done on the inside. Steve informed the phone people that the house would be ready for them on Thursday, but he was informed in return that there would be no technicians available for the outskirts of Acheron until Saturday, and the date was made for that day.

When they set out on that sun-drenched Monday morning, Steve Blair had the entire itinerary mapped out. "No rush," he said. He knew when and where they would stop for meals, and where they would sleep over. He planned the trip for a leisurely three days. "If we were in a hurry we could make much better time, but we aren't in a hurry, are we?"

"No hurry at all," Laura said.

"We're not a train, a plane, a Greyhound bus. We don't have to deposit people and pick up people on schedule, if you know what I mean. You know what I mean?"

"I know what you mean," Josh said.

"I want us to enjoy, take in the scenery, you know, all of that. Anytime you want to stop and look around, just say the word. If you get hungry, just say the word, but I don't think you're going to have to say any of those words. I've got three square meals planned for us every day, and good clean beds for us to sleep at night. Same as every summer. No different just because we're moving to Maine for a whole year. Same kind of trip—three squares in the daytime, and a good bed for a good sleep at night. Any questions?"

"No," Josh said.

"You're beautiful, dad," Laura said.

"You are the greatest," Josh said.

He was an unflappable driver, cool. He did a steady fifty on the good roads and reduced it to forty on the poor roads. There were no swerves, no veers, no tailgating, no sudden stops. He chatted with the kids and when they were not napping they chattered back.

Maureen looked at him, pretending to be looking past him, remarking on the passing scene on that side. He was still a handsome man, despite the circles under his eyes, and the small tic he had developed at the left corner of his mouth. The black hair was still jet black, with but a touch of gray at the temples; in all he was still that selfsame swarthy man that had caused her, so long ago, to dye her hair ash blond.

Because of the children.

And because of the questions people constantly asked, however innocently, pleasantly, but inexorably . . .

Of course the children knew they were adopted. Dr. Sam had advised that they be told as early as possible, but subtly, gradually, bit by bit at propitious moments. They knew that Jack and Nina were dead, and that Steve and Maureen had taken over as their adoptive parents, and they had grown into it without trauma. The difficulty came from the outside, from pleasant smiling people who never ceased asking those pleasant, smiling, innocent, but awfully awkward questions.

The reason: the extraordinary beauty of these twins. They had light blond hair, white skin, huge pale blue eyes: they looked like a pair of angels. Twins often cause comment, but extraordinarily beautiful twins never fail to cause comment. Unfortunately the unfailing comment, although always complimentary, was also always distressing.

"But they don't look at all like you people."

"They're towheads, and your husband is so dark!"

"And you a flaming redhead!"

In point of fact the kids looked a good deal like a combination of the Blairs—Steve's nose and forehead, Maureen's chin and shape of face (and Maureen did have blue eyes)—but it was the coloration, that extreme differential, that unsettled the innocent strangers (and their remarks were unsettling to the children). Josh and Laura were white-skinned blonds; in contrast Steve was dark complexioned and Maureen was a vivid redhead. "There's nothing I can do about me, but you *can* do about you," Steve said. "I dearly love that ruby red crown of glory around your head which I, as your husband, know is natural color—hell, I've seen the

43

matching collar and cuffs, as it were—but it's got to go. For the sake of the kids—gotta go. You've got to dye it blond, all the way—platinum blond. It might do the trick."

She did it all the way, almost as white blond as the kids, and it did do the trick. The disconcerting comments ceased; in fact, the next series of innocent strangers regularly remarked—but always when Maureen was present—upon the extraordinary resemblance between the beautiful twins and their beautiful parents.

The Ford station wagon rolled into the town of Acheron Falls at nine o'clock on Thursday morning. "Should we take her in to the doctor?" Steve asked.

"Don't be silly," Maureen said. "It's too early, it's not yet office hours, we didn't call for an appointment, and it's certainly no emergency."

"Certainly not," Laura said nasally.

On the trip, Laura had developed sniffles.

"Jeepers, dad, not to worry," Josh said.

"A little old summer cold," Laura said.

"Okay, all right, you guys," Steve said.

At reduced speed, twenty miles an hour, they drove along the main thoroughfare of Acheron Falls, population 9,114, which was not bad. The state of Maine, a large land mass of 30,920 square miles, had a gross population of only about a million people; its principal city had an approximate population of 62,000 souls; its next largest city boasted a populace of precisely 40,481; the next largest was about 31,000—and it went rapidly down from there. Jack Mercer, who had done studies, used to say that the average population of the various towns in the state of Maine was 800.

The main thoroughfare of the township of Acheron Falls comprised four blocks of paved streets and wide sidewalks, and the Ford station wagon passed a church, a hospital, a school, a doctor's office, a drugstore, the City Hall, the police station, a pool hall, a library, a movie theater, a beauty parlor, a bank, a supermarket . . . and there Steve parked the car and Maureen went in to purchase fresh staples—milk, eggs, ham, bacon, beef, bread, butter, cereal—to supplement the many cans of food they had in cartons. And then they were out on the highway at good speed, and then Steve slowed again as he made a turn into dirt roads. The house was fifteen miles and a half hour's drive from the town proper; Steve made a sharp left around a bend and there it was, sudden, gaunt, alone on a small rise of hill and stark against the sky.

It was a large house, even tall, but it had fewer rooms than one would imagine when viewing it from the outside, and there was good reason: every room, and the garage, was high-ceilinged, broad and wide and spacious. It was a wooden house, two-storied: ten rooms including the garage. It had a basement (called a cellar in Maine) which occupied all of the house underneath, and it had an attic which occupied all of the house on top.

It faced west.

There were five rooms, including garage, at ground level.

And there were five rooms, exactly above, on the second floor.

Downstairs, all the way to the left, was the garage. Above the garage, and the largest single room in the house, was Josh's bedroom, which was also his chemical laboratory.

Downstairs, to the right of the garage, was the living room (called the parlor in Maine). It had a small square vestibule, necessary because the entrance door of the house opened upon that room. Above the parlor was the master bedroom; it had once been Maureen and Steve's bedroom; it was now Steve's alone.

Downstairs, to the right of the parlor, was the kitchen; above the kitchen was Maureen's bedroom. Downstairs, to the right of the kitchen, was the dining room; above the dining room was the room Jack Mercer had used as a study: it had a stairway that led up to the attic. Downstairs, to the right of the dining room, was the recreation room; above the recreation room was Laura's bedroom, the brightest room of the house, southwest exposure. Laura loved it; even as a child she had demanded it. Laura loved the light, the setting sun, the last lingering glow in the sky.

Steve Blair pushed the button of his remote-control gizmo and the garage door rolled up, and the Ford purred up the gravel roadway and into the garage. Maureen, keys in hand, got out of the car and unlocked the door between garage and house.

"Josh," Steve said.

"Yessir?" the boy said.

"You and me, we'll do the rest of it. The ladies—mother and Laura—as of now they start opening up the inside of the house. You and me, we pull the stuff from the car and cart it in, and when we get it all in, then you and me, we do the unpacking, but if I know Laura—and I know Laura—she will do the directing."

The women carried in Maureen's supermarket purchases; the refrigerator was in excellent working order. Laura went out of the kitchen and through the parlor to the open door inside the garage and called to the men. "First you guys will bring in the cartons for the kitchen, which mother and I will unpack and put away. Then you guys—you men—can do all the rest. Okay?"

"Did I tell you who'd be the director?" Steve said.

"You didn't really have to tell me, did you?" Josh said.

By one o'clock most of the work was completed, and Maureen and Laura had done their share despite the negative chauvinistic remarks from father and son. "Pay them no heed, Laurie," Maureen said. "They knock the ladies in order to boost their own morale. They are sagging, they are tired; they've been working really hard."

"She's right," Steve said.

"I'm not sagging, I'm not tired," Josh said.

46

"No. The other thing—knocking the ladies. We have been doing that, and we're darn wrong to do it."

"Jeeps, we've been kidding, having fun."

"As long as that's clear to one and all," Steve said.

The cartons, stuffed with trash, were laid on the concrete walk on the north side of the house. That side also had the sunken holes that contained the garbage cans. Once a week—once they were notified—the trucks of the sanitation department of the township of Acheron Falls picked up trash and garbage; the Blair house, once the Mercer house, although fifteen miles from the center of town, was nonetheless within the legal perimeters set forth on the moldy maps that were piled on the shelves of the county clerk's office; the Blairs paid taxes to the city hall of the town of Acheron Falls and they were therefore entitled to all benefits, emoluments and services that the town provided to its taxpayers. Steve Blair had notified the sanitation department and there now would be regular trash-and-garbage pickups every Wednesday afternoon.

At two o'clock—four hours work with four people pitching in—they were finished. Everybody went up for showers and then came down to the kitchen for a meal of ham and eggs and hamburgers and biscuits and butter and English muffins, and then the kids went out to the back yard—a half acre enclosed within a chain-link fence—and Steve went up to the study to read, and Maureen—a fighter in the women's movement and a paid-up member of NOW—cleaned up the kitchen and did the dishes. She thought about coffee, but first sat down to rest near the breeze from an open screened-in window, a back window, and she saw the kids out there playing hardball catch, each of them equipped—gifts from Steve—with big-league-type baseball gloves.

God, they were beautiful.

God, if only Jack and Nina could see them now.

They were tall and strong and lithe, and no longer chil-

dren. They had come to puberty early, recently, at the beginning of twelve years old, gliding into it naturally, without
psychological pinch, no anxiousness, thanks to the brilliant
Steve Blair and, modestly, Maureen Blair. Sex education.
The Blairs' kids had learned it all, slowly, easily, all the way
from childhood, and when they arrived at puberty they
knew it all, knew what to expect; Josh and Steve had a long
talk and a few laughs; Maureen's talk with Laura was
somewhat more serious because Maureen instructed Laura,
without embarrassment on either side, in the techniques of
the menstrual pad and warned her (again) of the possibility
of menstrual pain (which did not happen to Laura Mercer
Blair). And that was it, that had been all of it for Josh and
Laura at puberty—no panic, no fright, no secret culs-de-
sac—and now there they were out there . . .

Baseball. They were baseball people like their father and
mother, Laura a Yankee fan (like mother), Josh a Met fan
(like dad), and there they were out there playing hardball
catch with big-league gloves, a gorgeous couple of kids, faces
like angels, and long lean graceful bodies. Josh was quite
powerful, very strong, tall, hard, biceps bulging, and naked
except for swim trunks and sneakers. Laura was already
exquisitely shaped: small pointed breasts, a round behind,
full thighs and long legs; her flaxen hair, tied in a ponytail,
flowed to her shoulders. She was wearing a pink bandeau,
pink shorts and white sneakers . . .

They stopped their game and trotted in to the kitchen
through the rear door. Laura sneezed.

"She feels lousy," Josh said.

"I feel fine," Laura said.

Maureen put her lips to Laura's forehead. "you feel warm,
but not hot. Let's go find out."

Josh put the gloves and the baseball on a corner of the
kitchen table. "She quit. She said she was tired. She never
gets tired, so that's the proof on top of the sniffles and the
sneezes that she's sick. I'll wait here for the report."

"Report?" Maureen said.

"You're taking her up to take her temperature, aren't you?"

"And you'll wait here—in the kitchen?"

"Well, I'm hungry. I'll grab a bite."

Maureen grinned. "That's more like it." She rubbed his tousled towhead. "There's ham, there's bread, there's milk—whatever you like." And rubbed his head again. "I'll be down quickly as possible to deliver the report."

"Okay." He was on his way to the refrigerator.

"All right, young lady, let's go."

They trotted upstairs; in the hall they passed Steve in the study. He was slumped in a chair, his heels on a table, reading.

"Hi," they called to him through the open door.

"Hi," he called back to them.

Laura's room, now in late afternoon, was still bright with southwest sunlight. "I love it here," Laura said. "I'm glad we're going to be here for a year. I'd like to be here like forever. Maybe it's my karma to be, like, you know, a country girl."

"Karma, no less. Where'd you get *that*?"

"I read it in one of dad's books."

"Okay, karma, get yourself down on the bed."

The thermometer registered one hundred and two-tenths.

"You're not going to die, but it's been lingering and I think maybe we ought to check it out. I'll be going into town tomorrow for some shopping—fresh fruits, vegetables and stuff like that there—and you'll come with me. We'll go early, and from town we'll call Dr. Harrison's office and make the appointment and go see him. All right with you?"

"You're my mother, mother."

Maureen kissed her and gave her a Tylenol. "Rest," Maureen said. "Take it easy, hang around the bed till suppertime, okay?"

"Like I said, you're my mother, mother."

"I love you, Laurie."

Maureen went out, looked in on Steve and told him about the plans for tomorrow. "Fine," he said.

"For now, how would you like some coffee?"

"You just read my mind," he said, and returned to his book.

Downstairs in the kitchen she found Josh finishing a thick ham-on-white with milk. "How's Laurie?" he said.

"A hundred and two-tenths."

"Could be a low-grade flu," said wise old Josh. "Maybe you ought to check her out with Dr. Harrison."

"I'm going to do that. We're going into town tomorrow morning."

"Smart, that's smart," Josh said. He stood up from the table. "I need some matches. Where'd you put the matches?"

Maureen's chin moved up, but only a trifle. "Don't tell me you've secretly taken up smoking."

"Don't be silly," Josh said. She was a little bit afraid of him, especially when he used that tone of voice—grave, mature, severe—a voice that was years older than his years. "Matches . . . for the work upstairs," he said in that slow grown-up voice. "Chemistry, my chemistry experiments, the Bunsen burner; I looked, there aren't any matches up there."

"Sure." She opened a drawer, gave him three packets of matches. "Be careful," she said.

"You're telling *me*?" Now the grave voice was solemn, and somewhat scornful, and he had that right, because it was he who often lectured them on the theories of fire prevention, and on the dangers, the hazards and harrows and carnage of uncontrolled fire, flash fire, raging fire . . . Joshua Mercer Blair, by far the most stable of the Blairs, had that one (and only) idiosyncrasy, a phobia: fear of fire.

"I'm sorry," Maureen said.

"I'll be careful," Josh said.

"I know," Maureen said.

He kissed her. He was already as tall as she. He took the

50

matches, and took up the hardball baseball and the big-league baseball gloves and winked at his mother and waved an elbow and went out and left her in the kitchen.

She brewed the coffee, letting it drip into the heat-holding earthenware coffeepot; she laid cups and saucers on a tray, and sugar and cream and the earthenware coffeepot, and carried the tray upstairs to Steve and laid it on the table.

"Thanks," he said absently, his feet still up, his face down, reading the book.

She set a cup for him, a cup for her, and poured coffee.

"Would you answer the phone, please?" he said.

A shiver coursed through her. "Phone? What phone?"

He did not look up. His nose was in the book. "Jeez, the frigging phone, please. Answer it."

"What phone?"

"The goddamn phone. Are you deaf suddenly? What is it with you?"

His nose was down there in the book.

The back of her neck, sweating, was icy cold.

She wanted to say, "*Are you crazy?*" She didn't. She said, "There are no phones, Steve. We're not connected yet, remember?"

"You know, that's right." He smiled easily. He took his feet off the table, closed the book, put it aside. He sipped his coffee. She did not. She had been dying for coffee, but now she did not want it, she wanted nothing. It's this damned house, she thought. He said, "I would swear I heard a phone ring."

"Can't be," she said.

"I know," he said. Then he said, "You're the one suggested coffee."

She smiled. Badly. "That I did, didn't I?"

"So how come you're not drinking your coffee?"

"I'm drinking, I'm drinking," she said. But she did not drink.

"Hear it?" he said.

"*What?*" The house. It's the damned house, she thought.

"A phone. The sound of a ringing phone. Don't you hear it?"

"*No, I don't.*"

"Look," he said. He smiled pleasantly, sipped coffee. "Look, I know the phones aren't hooked up and therefore there can't be a ringing phone." He put down his cup and cocked his head. "But don't you hear it?"

"No."

"You don't hear anything?"

"No."

"Probably something with the wind. Air blasts running into each other and producing a sound. A phone. A ringing phone. Lord, don't you hear it?"

"No." It's got to be this damned house, she thought.

"Christ, I hear it clear as crystal. A ringing phone. It can't be a ringing phone because we are not connected. But that's the sound. It has to be air drafts, hitting corners, coming off crevices. Don't look so scared, for God's sake. It's perfectly normal."

"Normal? It's normal to hear a ringing phone where there cannot be any ringing phones?"

"The sound of a ringing phone, the *sound*, that's normal. How do you think all those wind instruments work—an oboe, a trumpet, a saxophone, a trombone, a clarinet; hell, bagpipes? Air. It's all air pushing through—being blown through—crevices, but specified crevices. The music philosophers can call those specified holes anything from fissures, scissures, splits, rifts, grooves . . . hell, whatever the hell. Point is, it's air—wind—pushing through, that creates the sound, normal sound, all the way from the fart of a tuba to the thin wail of a flute. What's been happening here is wind—a breeze, whatever—rushing through *un*specified crevices and creating the sound of a ringing phone. Normal. What's *not* normal is that I hear it and you don't. *Listen.* Don't you hear?"

"No."

"Beats me . . ."

"It's this house."

"Maury, please, don't start that again."

"This damned house."

"Okay, okay, I don't hear it anymore." He stood and smiled at her amiably. "It's gone. Whatever the hell those winds, they've shifted, they're hitting other crevices. No more ringing phone."

"I don't care about the explanation, the normal, the winds, the crevices. What I care about . . . *you* heard a ringing phone—call it the sound of a ringing phone—but I did not! By me that's eerie. That's never happened before, not to us. I still say it's this damned house, this goddamned house—"

"Now stop it. Please. Think of the kids, for God's sake. We're going to be here for a year. I wouldn't have come if I'd've known you still had this crazy house-stuff on your mind. The ringing phone thing—easy, a normal scientific explanation. Even for me hearing it and you not. Where I was sitting, I heard the sound . . . where you were sitting— winds, crevices, and all—it was blank . . . That sort of phenomenon has happened thousands of times." He pulled her up from her chair, held her close. "Please, Maury, we're going to be here a year, and the kids and all. I don't believe in spooks, and I thought I'd convinced you. Please, don't start up with this house business all over again." He kissed her ear. "*Please* . . ."

"Okay, all right," she said, and tried to shake it off, but somewhere deep inside her the old fear came alive again, stirring faintly, and would not be denied.

Four ∾

AT TWENTY after ten on Friday morning they were in the supermarket doing shopping, mother and daughter, both in slacks and T-shirts, their hair swept back in ponytails. Maureen had called from a pay phone and had talked with Esmeralda Prichard, Dr. Harrison's receptionist-nurse; their appointment was for eleven o'clock.

Now, at ten to eleven, two shopping trolleys heaped with groceries—fruits, vegetables, cheeses, meats and bottles and cans of various sizes—they sought the owner but found the manager, who was the owner's wife, Mrs. Dora Hubball.

"Well, I'll be dingdonged if it ain't Miz Blair. Well, hello and welcome back to Acheron Falls, and hello to you, Laura Blair. Well, look at you two. Laura all grown up and Miz Blair seems gettin' younger all the time. Well, I tell you, I would swear, if I didn't know better, that these two are sisters, by golly . . ."

"Thank you," Maureen said. "How's Nicholas?" Nick Hubball was the owner of the supermarket.

"Just fine and dandy," Dora said. "Somethin' I can do for you folks?"

Maureen pointed. "We have these two carts of stuff, a lot of it perishable, and we've an appointment with Dr. Harrison for eleven. I was wondering . . . could you put it away for us, refrigerated, till we come back and pick it up?"

"You bet. Anything else?"

"That's it, thank you."

"For what? Thank me for what?" Dora looked at her wristwatch. "Good-bye, you two."

Outside Maureen said, "Suppose we leave the car right here in the parking. I'd like to walk. All right with you?"

"Fine with me."

Laura was better. Early this morning she had said, "I really don't have to go to the doctor." And Maureen had said, "Let's check it out anyway. Furthermore, I'd like you to help with the shopping." And Laura had said, "Okay, mother."

Now she said, "Could you get that kind of service in New York City? I mean, like the supermarket puts your things away in the fridge because you're taking your daughter to the doctor. I mean, they wouldn't do it in New York, would they?"

"I wouldn't dare ask in New York."

"See why—karma—I want to be a country girl?"

The doctor's office was the ground floor of a flat two-story clapboard house; the doctor lived upstairs. Outside on the lawn the doctor's ancient shingle, hanging from the horizontal shaft of a thin metal hinging post, swayed slowly in the Maine breeze: A.J. HARRISON, M.D.

He was Alfred Jonas Harrison, ancient as his swaying shingle. He had been ancient twelve years ago, when he had driven the fifteen miles to minister to the mother and to the twins already born; the father, Jack Mercer, had been Nina Mercer's midwife. Frost-haired, leather-faced Dr. A.J. Harrison was tall and unbent and, at least up to last summer, sturdy as a pine tree. As was his receptionist-nurse, just as ancient but even sturdier, Miss Esmeralda Prichard—Miss Essie—thin as a rail, sharp as a nail.

The white button was on the right side of the door; the small print under the button said: PLEASE RING. Obediently Maureen rang, but she knew from experience that the small print under the button meant nothing. There was no answer: no buzzing, no clicks; there was silence. She turned the knob and they entered the doctor's waiting room, cool, quiet and empty except for Miss Essie in starched whites behind a small desk.

"How do, Miz Blair."

"How are you, Miss Essie."

"Just fine and dandy. And how're you, Miss Laura. You're the sick one, is what your momma said on the phone. You look just pert and dandy to me, but 'course I ain't the physician . . ."

"I'm just fine, really, Miss Essie."

"Won't you folks set down. Doctor's on long-distance, but you'll have your full half hour, I promise."

Well, a full half hour, Maureen thought. As Laura would say, it ain't New York. In Acheron Falls there were no crowded waiting rooms, there were sufficient doctors in ratio to patients and all the doctors in Acheron Falls—unheard of in New York City—made *house* calls.

"Please, folks, do set down," Miss Essie said and Maureen could have sworn she detected a naughty gleam in Miss Essie's eyes. They sat in strong solid chairs, Maureen seeking Essie's eyes again but not catching them, and then the far door opened and a man entered the waiting room and Maureen's mouth opened.

The man said, "Mrs. Blair? Laura?"

Maureen said, "We're waiting for Dr. Harrison."

The man said, "I am Dr. Harrison."

Essie Prichard, her old eyes naughty, said, "He is Dr. Harrison."

Maureen Blair said, "What's going on here?"

Dr. Harrison—the Dr. Harrison she knew—was an old man—slender, erect—whose office attire was white pants and white shoes and a white choke-collar physician's jacket, and invariably when he came out to greet you his stethoscope hung from his neck like a lavaliere, like a soldier's dog tag: an identification.

Not this one—who made her heart stop.

56

For the second time in thirty-two years—ruefully, she thought, that's a long time—a man made her heart stop.

This one, this Dr. Harrison, Essie said *he* was Dr. Harrison—slender, erect—was dressed in black pants and black shoes and a white turtleneck. He was tall, even taller than Steve; he had brown hair, neatly styled; he had brown eyes behind wire-rimmed aviator glasses; he had a short-clipped fashionable brown beard. And he had Steve's tone of voice: gentle, soft-pitched, quiet.

"Mrs. Blair," he said, "your Dr. Harrison retired last winter. He's in Florida, fishing, swimming and playing golf. I am my father's son. I was practicing medicine in Boston but when my father decided to retire, I decided to come home and take over his practice."

Maureen Blair did not ask why: that was none of her business. But Maureen Blair, always outspoken, asked, "Then why haven't you changed that shingle out there?"

"No reason to change. Dad's name is Alfred Jonas Harrison. My name is Alan Jonas Harrison. The shingle says: A.J. Harrison, M.D. We Down Easters, it's in our bones, we're trained from childhood to be thrifty." He smiled, he had bright white teeth. "What reason to change that shingle out there?"

"And what reason for this conversation in here?" Laura said.

"Shush," Maureen said, and looked embarrassed.

"I'm sorry, mother, but in this case I don't think I should shush. I mean it's my time, if you know what I mean. I mean I'm the patient, right?"

Dr. Harrison said, "I know someone who would love you very much."

"Now who would that be?" Laura said.

"Her name is Diana. My daughter. She's eleven and a half."

"I'm twelve."

"I know."

"How do you know?"

"Your file—in fact your family file—is lying on my desk. I looked it over, at least your part of it." He gestured toward the far door, to the consultation room. "Shall we?"

He took her history and wrote it on her sheet in the file. They went into the enamel white examination room—Maureen with them—and he did a thorough workup, and during it he whispered to her, "Ain't a darn thing wrong with you, Miss Blair."

"That's what I told mother."

"Well, I'm the doctor, and I'm telling you."

Back in the consultation room, he sat behind his desk and they sat in chairs facing him. "Your temperature's normal; your heart, lungs, everything, perfectly normal. There's a virus-type low-grade flu going around—"

"That's what my brother said."

"Your brother's a doctor?"

"My brother's a genius."

He smiled, tapped the file now closed, looked toward Maureen. "The twin brother?"

"That's the only one," Maureen said.

"Virus-type low-grade flu going around, and you went through it, Laura, and on the way you probably generated some pretty good antibodies. Nothing wrong with you now, you're one hundred percent, and you do *not* require any dosage of medicine. There are doctors—too many of them in the cities—prescribe medication to please the patient. Psychologically"—he was talking to mother and daughter—"patients feel deprived unless the physician writes a prescription and the physicians write and write and *write*—to please the patient and also to justify the fee . . . well, Miss Laura, you're discharged. You don't have to do bed rest, or drink a lot of liquids, or face east and breathe deeply, or take aspirin or anything. Except vitamins. I'm big on vitamins . . ."

"So are we," Maureen said. "We have, all of us, a full vitamin regimen."

58

"Then that's it. Patient discharged. I wish you and your family a healthy and happy summer in Acheron Falls."

"We'll be spending more than just this summer in Acheron."

"Oh?" He leaned forward.

"A full year. My husband and I—we're schoolteachers in New York—we've taken a sabbatical. We'll be here in Acheron for a year."

"Poses some problems," Harrison said. "The most important of which, naturally, the children. School. And I'm delighted to inform you that right here in Acheron we have one fine school system, and I ought to know. We have a five-member board of education and I'm chairman. My dad was chairman. Kind of runs in the family. When I got here and they learned I was interested they elected me. Now about your kids, the twins, for school, please do call me; if you don't, I'll call you. They'll have to take tests in order for us to know in what class they belong. We have facilities for them to take these tests during the summer. That way, when the fall semester opens, they're registered in their proper classes without delay."

"I appreciate your interest," Maureen said.

"Chairman of the board." He smiled, stood up, and they did. "You're going to be here for a year and you've just come. I realize you've a great deal to do, but do call me as early as you can on this school business. If it's done in the summer it'll make it so much easier for them in the fall."

"She'll call you," Laura said. "If she doesn't, *I* will."

"Good girl." He came around the desk and hugged her.

Maureen said, "Good-bye, Dr. Harrison. Thank you so much."

They shook hands. His hand was large and comfortable and it held hers warmly for moments longer than a normal handshake, and she held his.

"Okay, let's go," Laura said.

They walked back to the supermarket, packed their groceries into the car. They drove home in silence, unusual for them.

Once Laura said, "He's real nice, isn't he?"

"Yes, he is," Maureen said. She seemed lost in thought.

Dr. Alan Jonas Harrison sat at his desk in his office in a small state of shock. For the second time in his thirty-nine years a woman had made his heart stop. The first time had been in premed school when he had met Alice Webster; six months later he had married her. The second time was today, out of nowhere, out of the blue: Mrs. Maureen Kirby Blair.

He studied the sheets in the file open on his desk. She was thirty-two. The husband—Steven Blair—was fifty. A big difference in age there: eighteen years. The twins—Laura and Joshua—now twelve, had been born to Mr. and Mrs. Jack Mercer who eight years ago had been killed in an automobile accident; the Blairs had adopted the children. They were healthy, all of them—Steven, Maureen, Joshua, Laura—no chronic illnesses. The children had been born in that crazy old house, the old Mercer house. Before it was the Mercer house it had been, for as long as anyone could remember, the Barbour house, unsalable, a white elephant. When Alan Harrison was a kid, he and his cronies used to call it the haunted house, but not because of ghosts or spooks or any of that. It was because the house was so far away out there, and all alone, a dark towering silhouette against the sky; and because of its baroque construction. It was high and long but not wide, a strange soaring narrow rectangle: five massive rooms downstairs (one a garage) and five massive rooms sitting directly above the downstairs rooms . . .

Dr. Alan Jonas Harrison closed the file and closed his eyes . . .

He had done his premed at the University of Maine at Augusta and there he had met and married Alice Webster; then they had been students together at Harvard Medical School in Cambridge. His father had wanted him to practice in Maine; her father had wanted her to practice in Massachusetts; so they had taken and passed the state boards in both Maine and Massachusetts. After residency in Boston City Hospital they had decided on Boston, a wife-husband medical team, she a gynecologist, he an internist. They were both twenty-seven when Diana was born. She was their only child.

And then at age thirty-six Alice Webster Harrison was struck with her first serious illness, her first and last.

The oncologist informed the husband, Dr. Alan Harrison, and then, on Harrison's advice, the oncologist informed Dr. Alice Webster Harrison: carcinoma. It involved the pancreas and the liver. Prognosis: perhaps two years; at most, three. The oncologist said nothing about metastasis and suffering; they were doctors, they did not have to be told.

She was a strong woman, Alice Webster Harrison, stronger than her husband; he knew what he would have done in her situation: he would have gone to sleep with a lethal overdose of sleeping pills. Alice elected to face up and fight, and mercifully she died at the beginning of the pain, only six months after the final diagnosis.

He continued to practice medicine in Boston with dwindling enthusiasm. And continued to care for his daughter in Boston, as a single parent but fearful. Boston. He had once been fond of the city, now it intimidated him: the muggings, rapes, murders; he worried even in his sleep about Diana.

At heart he was a small-town boy; he had been reared in a town where people did not even lock their doors. Perhaps those days were over, perhaps these days they did lock their doors, but as his father told him whenever he came to visit in Boston, Acheron Falls was still clean and pretty, pristine—not filthy dirty like the big cities—and it still had all the Down East virtues and still had a tiny police department because there was so little crime, if any real crime at all, in the township of Acheron Falls in the great state of Maine, the Pine Tree State of the USA.

And then, last winter, when dad definitely said he was retiring, Dr. Alan Jonas Harrison—after consultation with his daughter—gave up his practice in the city of Boston and came home to Acheron Falls.

Where he had just met the only woman since his wife to make his heart stop.

Five ∾∾∾

THE MEN from the phone company, three young men, arrived at the Blair house at ten o'clock on Saturday morning. As Steve had originally ordered, there were new instruments to be installed. The main phone would now have extensions in the kitchen, the master bedroom (Steve), the bedroom next door (Maureen) and the study. There would be a new phone with a separate number for Laura in her room, and a new phone with a separate number for Josh.

At one o'clock the work was finished. Maureen offered lunch, the men politely refused. Steve signed their papers and they were gone.

It was a busy week, arranging, fixing, making a home. Curtains went up on windows, bed linens went onto beds, furniture was shifted, pictures were hung on walls. Steve's most prized picture was a cartoon, an original Jack Mercer, never published. It was one of those in the file that Jack had forgotten to pack eight years ago.

"A masterpiece," Steve had said when they had found it. "In this one Jack surpassed himself—in focus, composition, concept. I hereby lay claim to it."

Steve had had it lacquered for preservation and framed under glass, and it always hung in what he considered a place of honor. Now it was hanging, by itself, on a long wall in the study. It was a charcoal drawing, bold strokes, black on white. On top a man was flying upward, obviously distressed, his hands holding his buttocks. Under him—its expression bland, benign—was what looked like a horse with a pointed horn rising from the middle of its head. The caption: IT IS UNWISE TO PLAY LEAPFROG WITH A UNICORN.

"It says it all," Steve Blair said. "It even explains me— my alleged atheism, iconoclasm, why I don't go for anything that can't be scientifically proved. In that picture Jack Mercer says it all. If you fool around with the supernatural, with wild-out stuff like the mythical unicorn—watch out. Because in the end you're going to get it right up the ass."

At week's end things had begun to shape up and simmer down. Steve had driven Josh to Jackson City—forty-five miles away—where they had purchased chemicals and additional chemical apparatus (beakers, burettes, crucibles, pestles, funnels, test tubes) for Josh, and from a musty old bookstore, a number of interesting secondhand books for Steve. Jackson City, population 31,119, was the nearest "big city" to Acheron Falls.

Josh's bedroom was also his "lab." Situated directly over the garage, it was the largest room in the house. It had good light; there was a window to the north and a window to the front of the house, the west. The east wall had his workbench, his Bunsen burner, his Buchner funnel and the cabinets for his chemicals, books and chemical equipment. This room was now completely in order, as were all the other rooms—except the study. Steve had helped Josh with his room; Maureen had worked with Laura on hers. Laura's room, the brightest, was at the opposite end from Josh's and it also had two windows, one to the south and one to the front of the house, the west. For Laura's room, Maureen had selected the happiest pictures, the gauziest curtains and the prettiest bed linens.

The study still needed work, and the men did it. Steve's books were piled on the floor against the walls because there were not enough shelves to contain them. There were planks in the basement—and saws, nails, hammers, paints, brushes—and the men manufactured bookshelves for the study; the raw wood needed painting and Steve reserved that job for himself.

Every day now the family went swimming in their cove by the sea. They did not drive: it was a fifteen-minute walk to the white beach that lay within a U-shaped perimeter of large boulders and small rocks. They carried swimsuits and towels in duffel bags and changed out of sight of each other.

"We go out there for the fishing, Josh and I," Steve said, indicating the long ends of the U that jutted far out to sea like natural jetties. "But not yet. We're not ready yet for serious fishing. Serious fishing proscribes the presence of impatient women."

"There he goes again, our male chauvinist pork chop," Maureen said.

"Mother has a point there," Josh said gravely.

"Okay." Steve opened his arms and bowed. "I humbly beg everybody's pardon."

And they all ran into the sea, swimming lustily.

They were nut brown from the sun. They looked so healthy, it was shameful. Maureen had told Steve about the new Dr. Harrison and the board of education and the possibility of summer exams for the kids.

"Competency exams for grades," she said. "In Acheron Falls they're still called aptitude tests."

"By all means," Steve said.

She had called Dr. Harrison, he had called the school board and a date had been set for the fourth week in June.

Nut brown, except for the swarthy Steve, who was chocolate brown. There was a good deal of out-of-doors. When the family was not swimming at the cove (or working inside the house), they were playing baseball in the backyard, a four-person family game with a recondite system of individual point scores. There was a pitcher, a catcher, a batter, a fielder (each position regularly rotated) and there were only two bases: first and home.

The backyard was a half acre inside a high chain-link fence. The property, house and grounds, was four acres, but the Blairs maintained (as the Mercers before them) that half acre in back of the house and the front lawn; for the rest it was all tall grass and wild growth.

This day, after the baseball, Josh had called a friend in New York City, a long call, and Steve had delivered a lecture. "What you have to understand, Josh and Laura, you can't call your friends in the city and just talk and talk. You now have your own phones, like we began last year at home, but here it's different, from here to New York it's long-distance, and long-distance costs a lot of money. Some of your friends have rich parents who just don't give a damn—so, when you call your friends, tell them you have to keep it short, but if they want, and it's okay with their parents, they can call you back and talk as long as they like. Pretty soon you'll be having friends here in Acheron . . ."

Now the kids were out front mowing the lawn, and Maureen was sipping coffee in the study, watching Steve on his knees painting the bookshelves, his back to her.

"The phone," he said.

She put down the cup of coffee.

"Answer the phone."

She sat rigid. She was cold. It was as though a wind were whirling in the room. "No phone. There's no phone ringing."

He turned, still on his knees. His face was distorted. "Why are you playing games with me?" Suddenly there were tears in his eyes. "My God, Maury, do you want to drive me crazy? *Answer the phone.*"

"There is no phone—"

He stood up. "My God, don't you hear . . ."

She took his arm, led him firmly to the telephone. She picked up the receiver. "Now it can't be this one anymore, can it?"

"No."

"Is a phone still ringing?"

"Yes, and you know it."

She put the receiver back. She took his arm again, walked him out of the study and walked him to Josh's room. She plucked the receiver from the phone and held it up. "If it was this phone, I just broke the connection, right?"

"Right."

"Do you still hear . . . ?"

"There's a phone ringing." But his voice was less certain.

Once again she took his arm, and now she led him all the way across to Laura's room. She lifted the receiver from its cradle. "This is the last. There's only this one that could have been ringing. Please, are you convinced?"

His eyes blinked. "Yes," he said faintly.

"No more ringing?"

Now there was a change. An abrupt change. He seemed to be listening to something other than a ringing. He seemed to turn inward. His eyes grew crafty. "No more," he said, and smiled. But his smile was a cover-up.

"No more?" It was a prayer.

"My imagination," he said. "I'm a little nuts, you know. The goddamn nerves. Which is why we're here, for the sabbatical. I'm sorry to screw you around, Maury." And he smiled again, a broad smile. She didn't like it a bit. It was all teeth. A flinch of the lips and a show of teeth. "Let's forget it," he said, smiling.

"No more?" she said.

"Nothing," he said.

"All gone?"

"Absolutely all gone." But his voice was not his voice. Too harsh, nearly guttural.

"No more ringing? No more phones? Right now, no more? Right now this minute there's no phone ringing?"

"Nothing. It's over. All clear."

She knew he was dissembling. She knew Steve Blair. The strange crafty eyes, the voice that wasn't his voice, the smile that wasn't a smile—she knew he was lying.

She knew that right now, this minute, he did hear a phone ringing.

And it scared the hell out of her.

Six ∽∞∾

Josh Blair was a heavy sleeper. The boy slept like dead. His phobia was fear of fire, but his one idiosyncrasy was that deep sleep; it was as though he were in another world. An alarm clock did not waken him; nor even the screech of a police siren. To wake him before he came awake by himself, he had to be shaken, vigorously. In New York, in order to get him up for school, he was shaken vigorously by Maureen or Steve or even Laura, but more often than not he dropped back to sleep and had to be shaken all over again.

On this Thursday late in June they started shaking him at six o'clock in the morning; they were to take their aptitude tests at eight o'clock in the white brick school in Acheron Falls. And there was reason for that early hour.

Dr. Alan Jonas Harrison's office hours were ten to twelve, and then three to six; before, in between and after, he did his house calls. On this Thursday at eight o'clock he would be present in the white brick schoolhouse because he was interested in the new full-time students, but more, he was interested in their mother. When he had talked with her to make the appointment, he had told her he was making it early, before his office hours, because it would be of benefit if he were present: politics applies even to twelve-year-olds taking aptitude tests. Dr. Harrison proffered those hints over the phone, and Maureen understood. The tests took one hour; Dr. Harrison said he would be happy to sit in when the papers were being marked, which would be immediately after the tests were taken, and again Maureen understood.

What Dr. Harrison did not say, and therefore Maureen did not know, was that he planned—during the hour that the kids were taking their tests—to sit around somewhere with Maureen and get better . . . acquainted with her.

It took a half hour from the house to the town. Maureen had begun to time herself. Aside from shopping, and whatever other reason she had to go into town during the summer, with the start of school in September she would be making the trip twice a day, chauffeuring the kids into town and then picking them up to drive them home. In normal weather and at normal speed, it was a half-hour trip.

On this Thursday she got them to the schoolhouse at ten minutes to eight, and there outside, tall in the sunshine, stood Dr. Alan Jonas Harrison.

He waved. "Hi," he said as they approached.

Maureen introduced him to Josh.

"A handsome blue-eyed towhead, just my daughter's type," Harrison said. "Beware, young man; she's going to fall madly in love with you."

"Thank you, sir," Josh said.

"Good luck on your tests, you two."

Harrison ushered them into the schoolhouse, and came out to Maureen Blair.

They sat on a bench in the sunshine in a small green park. Maureen was confused and worked hard to hide it. She was in love, or whatever the modern word for her agitation was. For the second time in her life she had gone nutsy—immediately, incomprehensibly—with a stranger, and she was still married to the man with whom it had happened the first time. Once, okay, possible, it can happen once. But twice like that . . . ? She consoled herself with the thought of the time lapse in between, almost thirteen years; the first time she had been twenty years old; now at her next birthday she would be thirty-three. And there had been the pressure with Steve, her own pent-up needs . . .

". . . and therefore I postponed all of this morning's appointments," Alan Harrison was saying. "Don't have to be in the office until three. That's not usual for me, but things haven't been quite usual for me since the day you and Laura . . ."

Was he declaring himself, or was she reading into what he was saying? Was she spinning a love at first sight scenario for *both of them*? Was he saying by signal, by innuendo, what he could not dare say outright? Ridiculous, she thought. We've only met once before this, and I'm a properly married woman and he is a proper small-town doctor. He is a good, kind man and he is helping the new woman in town and her children—her adopted children—who were born out there in the old Mercer house, and his father was the doctor who attended—

"Coincidence," he was saying.

"I beg your pardon?"

"Coincidence," he repeated. "One of those well-endowed foundations should do a study, as scientific as possible, on the mysteries of coincidence. All my life I've been haunted by coincidence; and my patients regularly tell me tall tales of incidents of coincidence. It happens to all of us, don't you think?"

"All the time," she said.

"My daughter Diana was born on the second day of the month—month of September. Your kids were born on the second day of a month—April. Diana was born at 3:16 A.M. in Saint Elizabeth's in Boston on September second. Your kids were born five months before and within that same hour, according to my father's records, but certainly on the second day of the month, April second. With your kids there's no precise record of the minute of birth—"

"They weren't born in a hospital."

"I know."

"They're not my—my biological children."

"I know. But the coincidence of day of the month and time of the day—"

71

"Are you, a physician, into astrology?"

"I do charts."

She laughed. "So do I."

"I can't say that I believe, but it amuses me—"

"My husband hates it."

"Each to his own." He sat back on the park bench. "On the other hand, there is a divergence. Diana, who in a few months will be twelve, is still prepubescent and that by a long shot. I don't think she'll come into puberty until thirteen; maybe even later."

"Well, I was fourteen . . ."

"But Josh and Laura—"

"Within days of their twelfth birthday."

"Genes," Harrison said. "It's a matter of the genes." He looked off and smiled and called, "Well, look who's here."

The girl came to them, a slender girl with long brown hair, an oval face and big brown eyes.

"Diana!" he said.

"Daddy, stop it," she said. "Stop sounding so surprised." She grinned. She had bright white teeth, like her father. "You told me to be here, and you told me when to be here—and here I am."

"Want you to meet Mrs. Blair," he said. "Maureen Blair, Diana Harrison."

"I'm pleased to meet you," Diana said.

"Me too," Maureen said.

"My daughter," he said.

"I'm sure she knows that," Diana said.

"Her kids'll be out soon," Harrison said.

Diana said to Maureen, "They're doing those darn aptitude tests, aren't they?"

"Yes."

"Pain in the backside," Diana said. "I had to do them too, and quicklike, because it wasn't summer vacation; it was wintertime."

"How'd you make out?"

"Okay. Got assigned to the grade where I belonged." And

again that bright white grin. "But what you must remember, my gramps was then the chairman of the board of education. Now it's my dad, which, I hope, will just the same help your kids."

"Laura and Josh," Harrison said. "You'll love them, Di."

"I'm sure I will," Diana said, and smiled her smile of the innocent.

The kids came out at ten minutes after nine. Harrison introduced them to Diana, and then he disappeared into the schoolhouse. "How was it?" Maureen asked.

"Okay," Josh said.

"Fine," Laura said.

"Don't worry at all," Diana said. "My dad's in there and he's a big shot with the board. Nobody's going to do you wrong."

Maureen laughed. Josh moved about studying the birds in the trees. But Laura and Diana studied each other and quickly took to each other. Maureen was, of course, delighted. Then Diana said, "We're getting company."

He was a tall man; he walked with a magisterial stride. He was dressed in khaki and he wore a broad-brimmed, high-crowned cowboy hat, an expensive Stetson. He had a huge belly around which was strapped a gun belt, the holster hanging over his right hip. He was Marcus Nolan, the chief of police of Acheron Falls. He came up to them and tipped his hat.

"Howdy, Miz Blair, and welcome back to Acheron Falls. Howdy, Miss Laura. Howdy, Mr. Joshua. And howdy to you, Miss Diana. Would you know where you dad's at? He ain't at home or in the office."

"Schoolhouse," Diana said. "He's in there helping mark papers."

"When he comes out would you tell him to come over see me at the station house."

"Okay, Chief Nolan."

"I think it would be wise if you all came along with him."

He touched the brim of his hat in a small salute. "Thankee. A good day to you." He turned on his heel and strode off.

At ten o'clock a beaming Dr. Harrison joined them in the park. "Congratulations." Solemnly he shook hands with Laura and then with Josh. "Flying colors," he said. "I didn't do a thing in there except sit and listen to them praise you. They agree with New York; you're a couple of real smart kids. You'll be in exactly the same grade as you would have been in New York City, which is the same as Diana here. What I did do—I made sure you'd all be in the same class."

"Good!" Diana said. "Thank you. I love that."

The girls embraced. Josh smiled.

Maureen said, "Chief Nolan passed the time of day with us."

"Nolan? What's he doing in our little park?"

"Looking for you, daddy," Diana said. "He saw me and came over to ask. He said he tried you at home and in the office. I told him you were in the school. He said for you to go and see him in the station house. He said for us to come with you."

Harrison looked toward Maureen.

"That's the message," Maureen said.

"Okay, then," Harrison said. "Let's go get arrested."

It was a short walk, but hot.

"It's gonna be a scorcher," Josh said.

The station house was white brick, like the schoolhouse. Inside a young officer said, "Hi, doc. Go right in. He's waitin' on ya."

"All of us?"

"You bet."

The chief's office was a large room, cool and quiet. He was seated behind his desk, his Stetson on his head, his gun belt around his belly, his gun in its holster. He said, "Good of you to come, doc." He opened a drawer and took out a rolled-up picture, the size of a poster. He stood up, unrolled the picture and tacked it to a cork board on a wall. "This

74

came in this mornin'. Figgered I'd talk to you first, then put it up outside for everybody to get a good look. Remember him?"

"Mitch Ranson." Harrison's voice was dead serious.

Chief Nolan said, "Take a good look, all of you."

The man in the picture had broad shoulders and a thick neck. He was bald in front; for the rest, his hair was black. His nose was broken like the nose of a prizefighter, and there was a scar on his right cheekbone.

"Mitch Ranson," the chief said. "He grew up in this town; he was a friend of doc's when they was growin' boys. Doc went to school in Massachusetts, but Mitch got a scholarship to USC becuz he was a terrific football player. Got that nose busted playin' football, and also that scar on his cheek, and also got hit in the head too much, which musta made him go bananas—"

"No, that's not fair, Marcus."

"Well, then, maybe it was the disappointment becuz he could not make it as a pro. Or maybe he could not make it as a pro becuz by then there was already some screws loose in his head. He came home to Maine and went to work as a football coach in a high school in Portland, and a year later all the screws came loose in his head and he was a hunnerd percent a crazy. Is *that* fair, Alan?"

"Yes."

"Killed a man in Portland, for no reason, just a frenzy. Next he was heard of in Southern California. Stayed over with friends, a family, and in the mornin' two of them was dead, smashed to pieces, and Mitch was gone. By then the word was out on Mitch to cops all over the country; they was lookin' for a hunnerd percent bonkers looney-bird dangerous; a homicidal maniac. Right, Alan?"

"Yes."

"Came back to Maine, killed a guy in Bangor, killed a guy in Lewiston, and when they caught up with him and captured him he had just bashed in a guy's brains on a beach in Westbrook. He did not even have to stand trial, he was a raving lunatic. They took him outa society. They put him away for good and all in Portland in a facility for the criminal insane and locked the door on him. So, guess what? Three days ago he got out—escaped. And now there's an all-points out for him all over the state of Maine, and this mornin' we got these posters to hang up in case anybody should happen to see him—anywhere in the state of Maine. That's why you, Miz Blair, and the kids are lookin' at that poster. If you should see anywhere anybody looks even a little bit like him—you call it in to this here office. Right?"

"Yes," Maureen said.

"Right, kids?"

"Yes," they said.

"You think, doc, he might come back here?"

"No," Harrison said. "Why should he?"

"Hell—he was born here, got raised here."

"There'd be nothing for him to come back *to*. His parents are dead. There were two sisters and they moved away from Acheron Falls long ago; they're both married. One lives in San Diego, the other one in Montreal."

"But it's *possible* he'd come back here?"

"No more possible than he'd go to Southern California."

"But it *is* possible. I mean everything's *possible*."

"Yes, chief, everything is possible."

"Since he was born here and raised here, the state police want me to do a write-up on him, like a profile, y'know, and who better to help me on that than Dr. Alan J. Harrison, who knew the subject from boyhood on. Willya kindly help me on that, doc?"

"Yes, but on one proviso."

"Proviso?"

"Let's release these prisoners. May I go out with them and send them off—including my daughter—to wherever they may wish to be sent off to?"

"Yes, sure, I'm sorry," Chief Nolan said, and did a smart salute against the brim of his Stetson.

A nice fella, Dr. Harrison thought, but just a little hard to take seriously.

Outside, Harrison took Maureen aside. "Best laid plans of mice etcetera. I'd arranged to be free until three." He touched her hand. "I know I'm not entirely making sense, but . . . I had hoped we might sort of sit around and talk. But now this Mitch Ranson business, the write-up for the state police . . ."

"I understand." And she did, in more ways than one . . . It seemed to be happening for him too . . .

The children came to them.

"Please, Mrs. Blair," Diana said.

"Yes, dear?"

"Can Laura stay, like overnight? I like her a lot and she likes me and I've been lonely here, Mrs. Blair. I'm a new-comer, and the kids in this town, they're kinda standoffish. Now Laura's here, and she's a newcomer, and like that we're a pair . . ."

"How about it, mother? I'd love it."

"You don't have clothes. You're not prepared—"

"Mrs. Blair, I have enough clothes for the two of us. *Please?* There's so much Laura can do here in town, so much I can show her, so much the two of us can do together . . ."

"Tomorrow?" Maureen said. "How about tomorrow? It's Friday. How about, look—the weekend?"

"Great," Laura said.

"Oh, I'd love that," Diana said.

"She can prepare, pack her things, all of it, the weekend— that is, if we have Dr. Harrison's permission."

Which of course they did.

When they got home the sun was in the middle of the sky. "We got us a scorcher," Josh said, and looked around for his father and did not find him. "Dad's no dope," Joshua said. "This kind of day, not knowing when we'd get home, he's out at our cove, and we're going to join him—"

"Not me," Maureen said. "I'm bushed."

"Would you make us some eats to take?"

She prepared sandwiches and placed them into a portable cooler with bottles of soft drinks. Laura showered and re-dressed in light clothes, as did Josh. They stuffed their swim togs into a canvas duffel bag and added towels, unguents, blankets and a radio. Josh carried the canvas bag, Laura carried the portable cooler and Maureen waved good-bye to them, and only then did the pangs cut through: she was ravenously hungry.

She made coffee. She toasted English muffins, buttered them lavishly and added grape jelly. She cooked an omelet of three beaten eggs with minced ham and onions, and she was in the midst of her sumptuous meal when the refrigerator disturbed her.

What was it?

What was wrong?

There was nothing wrong with the refrigerator.

It was what was *not* wrong that disturbed her.

Nothing hung on the door of the refrigerator. There was no note, no communication attached by Scotch tape. That was what was wrong. Steven Blair would never go off on his own, his family away, without leaving a note telling of the what and when and where.

It stopped her in the middle of the meal. She stood up uneasily, peering about the kitchen as though half expecting that someone—or something—would leap out at her from the shadows. Nothing leaped at her.

She went out to the backyard: perhaps he was asleep in the sun. There was no one in the backyard. Then perhaps he was napping upstairs in his bedroom. She returned to the house and checked the master bedroom: it was empty. Now resolutely, starting with the basement, she trudged from room to room, every room in the house—nothing.

She sipped cold coffee in the kitchen. Perhaps he *had* gone off—fishing or swimming or whatever—without, this once, leaving a note on the fridge. There was still the attic, but her heart was no longer in it. It was a nice attic—not dim, creepy, cobwebby. It was a long, clean, narrow room; daylight came in through the two ventilation grates at either end; there were no windows, but there were electric lights for when it grew dark, the switch just inside the doorway. The Mercers had put down a vinyl flooring and had papered the walls with gay designs; it had been the twins' favorite room when they were small. Now it contained everything that had belonged to the kids when they were growing up— their toys, their little tables and chairs, Josh's trains, Laura's dolls, baby clothes . . . it was a room of mementos.

She poked a fork at the half-eaten ham omelet and then, determinedly, started for the attic—because she could not do otherwise. It was ingrained, an integral part of her nature, a precept taught by her father: always finish what you begin. The stairs to the attic were in the hallway just outside the study: seven steps up and then a small square vestibule and then the door. She fairly ran upstairs and up the stairs to the attic: she wanted to get it over with. She wrenched open the door . . . and froze.

He was sitting on the floor, facing her.

He did not see her: his eyes were vague.

He was sitting cross-legged, Indian fashion, with a little red phone in his lap, the receiver pressed close to his left ear. She recognized the little red phone. It was a sturdy toy telephone that had once belonged to four-year-old Josh. Now Steve squeezed his eyes closed: he was straining to hear. Then quite suddenly, unhappily, he slammed down the receiver. He opened his eyes. He looked at her absently. His voice was thin. "He's trying to say something to me, but it won't come through, it's too faint, he's been dead too long."

She managed to say, "Who?"

"Jack Mercer. Who did you think?"

Oh my God.

Seven ∽◦◦◦∼

ON FRIDAY at eleven-thirty Maureen Blair was driving Laura to her weekend with Diana Harrison, and Josh was in the car with them. Josh had wanted to spend the weekend in Acheron Falls, not because of Diana, but because it would be an adventure to stay there in the heart of the town and learn about it. It was not because of Diana. He had no interest in Diana and, no matter Dr. Harrison's nice compliments, Diana had no interest in him.

Maureen had jumped at the chance: she wanted the weekend alone with Steve. She had called Dr. Harrison, and of course Josh was invited to stay the weekend. Now the kids, with bags packed, were on their way, and Maureen was on her way, ultimately, to a conversation with Dr. Samuel Vaughn.

She had gotten nothing from Steve. She had helped him to his feet and he had put away the toy phone on a shelf in the attic. "What was *that* all about?" she had asked.

He had done his best grin for her. "It was me being nutty, and I admit it. Honey, I'm in the midst of a nervous breakdown, remember? Why don't you back off and let me enjoy it." But there was that crafty look in his eyes again. He was skirting around her: he wanted her out. Whatever it was that was happening to him, he was trying to keep her out of it. Since that day when she had led him from phone to phone to convince him there was no ringing, since that day when his eyes had first grown crafty, and his smile was not really a smile . . .

The kids rushed to each other and went off happily, Josh included. "Delightful, aren't they?" Harrison said. It was twelve o'clock: he had no appointments until three.

"May I use your phone?"

"Sure."

"Not the office phone, the house. I'm going to call New York. I'll pay the charges, of course."

"Forget the charges." But his frown was a question.

"I can't make this call from home." She didn't want it to show on the telephone bill. Later she would have to explain it to him, and inside her she was glad of that.

"This way." He led her upstairs to a phone alone. "I'll be waiting in our park," he said.

She dialed Dr. Samuel Vaughn and got him: it was almost his lunch hour, he was not with a patient. "If you were," she said, "I'd have had your service cut in and put me through—emergency."

He said calmly, dear Dr. Sam, "We have an emergency?"

She told him all of it: the phantom ringing phones. And then she told him about that day when Steve was painting the shelves, when he heard the ringing, when she led him from telephone to telephone, and the peculiar look came into his eyes. "That was when he put me out of it. He no longer talked to me about ringing phones." And then she told him about yesterday, the scene in the attic with the little red phone, and how Steve had laughed it off and had told her to let him enjoy his nervous breakdown.

"That's it," she said. "That's my story, doc."

There was silence on the other end.

"Sam?"

"I'm here."

"What do you think?"

"What do *you* think?"

"I—I think he's hallucinating. It's not that he *sees* things. But can there be . . . ?"

"Yes, there can be. Aural hallucinations."

But the way he said it, his tone of voice, it held her down, somehow it calmed her.

"How's he been—otherwise?"

"Aside from a little matter of aural hallucinations?"

"Temporarily. How's he been?"

"As they'd say here in Acheron Falls—just fine and dandy. Resting, reading, swimming, hiking. He *looks* terrific. He's gained a little weight and that tic he used to have—it's gone. I guess you could say he's quite remarkably improved."

"Bed?"

"Pardon?"

"Sex?"

"He's not that remarkably improved."

"Nothing?"

"Nothing at all."

"All right, back to aural hallucinations," he said. "It's not an infrequent phenomenon at the tail-end of a severe depression. It should pass. If you want, I can arrange that he be hospitalized . . ."

"Is it necessary?"

"Not at all."

"Then I don't want."

"Good girl. Now listen. This thing should run its course and disappear, but you stay with him, stay on his side, don't fight him. If you reestablish confidence, he'll confide in you. If you coddle him, cozzen him, then if and when he hears the ringing again, he'll talk to you about it, he'll tell you. It's possible it's over; possible there won't be any more. If so, the aural hallucinations have been the fever pitch, the crisis, and once over that hump the patient shakes off the depression and is on his way to recovery. Like the crisis—the high-fever pitch—in physical illness."

"Do you think . . . ?"

"I don't know, but you stay right in there with him. If he's better you'll know it soon enough. If not, if the ringing starts again, at least he'll know you're with him, on his side, and he *will* confide in you, and that's good, an integral part of recovery. He will talk it out with you, through you, and in time it should dissipate. He will want to talk, Maureen; he needs to confide in a friend. Not an antagonist. Be on his side, show him you're on his side, and he'll talk to you, and if he can talk it out, all of it—it'll go away."

"Are you sure?"

"In my business, dear Maureen, I'm afraid we aren't sure of anything." A moment's pause, then he said, "What's your number?"

"Pardon?"

"Your phone up there?"

She gave him the telephone number. "But don't call," she said. "I'm using an outside phone. He doesn't know and I don't want him to know . . ."

"Very good. But you keep calling, please. Let me know what goes on. Chin up. We love you, Maureen."

"We love you, Dr. Sam. Good-bye. God bless."

He was waiting in their little park, the tall slender man with the clipped brown beard and the soft brown eyes behind the wire-rimmed aviator glasses. He stood up as she came to him. "You okay?" he said.

"Just fine and dandy," she said. It made her laugh.

He took her hand, drew her down to the bench and kept her hand. "Just fine and dandy," he repeated, and shook his head.

"The call to New York," she said. "Don't get ideas. It wasn't to a lover, nothing that romantic. A friend of ours, a psychiatrist." Abruptly, she pulled her hand from his. "My husband," she said. "He's been having difficulties. Oh, quite minor. Sort of—a depression. We decided on a sabbatical. It's why we'll be here for the year. Anyway, I wanted to talk to our friend, his shrink, but I didn't want Steve, my husband, to know, didn't want him to worry, to magnify . . ."

"I understand." And he changed the subject. "How about lunch. You hungry?"

"Yes, I'd like lunch. Where?"

"I know a place . . ."

They drove in his car a few miles out of town to a farmhouse. "It's an inn, actually," he told her. "Owned by a woman I've known all my life, Clare Selwyn. When her husband died, Clare became an innkeeper. She took in a few lodgers and then branched out. She's a wonderful cook."

Clare Selwyn was a small woman with white hair, a round rosy face and a smile with dimples. "Alan! It's so good to see you."

He kissed her, introduced her to Maureen.

"My pleasure," Mrs. Selwyn said. "It's too nice a day for you people to dine indoors. Come, please. This way."

She guided them to a table, out of the sun, under a huge tree. "Lovely," Maureen said. "This is just lovely."

Mrs. Selwyn recited the menu, and they ordered. When she went away, Harrison said, "I'm not due back in the office until three, and I've no house calls to make. We've lots of time, and I can assure you that Clare won't rush us."

They had Maine clam chowder, striped bass ("fished up this mornin'") with two vegetables ("picked fresh today"), and apple pie ("baked by me, personal") and coffee.

And they sat there in the cool fragrance of Maine summer, and talked. The talk was their bridge, it linked them, and they held on, talking compulsively. He avoided mention of Steven Blair and sedulously avoided any mention of mental illness, psychiatrists and sabbaticals. They talked, crossing and recrossing their bridge, of many minor matters, of movies and TV and sitcoms and plays and books and favorite authors; they talked about Boston, about New York, about their children, about the psychology involved in raising children; and they talked about such other minor matters as presidents and politics and superpowers and nuclear war.

She was like a schoolgirl, only what she felt was hardly girlish.

She was also a Catholic lady, feeling this way about a man who was not her husband. Bad enough, but worse—she was still in love with the sick man who was her husband.

She came home at four o'clock. In the car she pushed the button of the electronic gizmo; the garage door rolled up and she returned the gizmo to the glove compartment. She drove into the garage; in moments, the garage door rolled down. She entered the house though the connecting door from the garage to parlor. "Steve!" she called.

No answer.

She went to the study and then to his bedroom: he was not home. It was too late for swimming, or solitary fishing; he was probably out there somewhere in the countryside, walking, trudging, thinking, kicking stones. She was glad. For now, she was glad. For now she was glad to be home alone.

In her room she undressed and showered; then she lay, uncovered, on top of the bed. It was hot summer. She lay, spread-eagled on top of the bed, her hands clasped behind her head. She had wanted this weekend, the kids gone, alone with him. Try to have him confront his hallucinations. Challenge him . . . but no more, not after her talk with Dr. Sam. Now it was her job, according to Dr. Sam, to stay with him, stay on his side. "Don't fight him," Sam had said. "If you reestablish confidence, he'll confide in you . . . he will talk it out with you, through you and in time it will dissipate . . . Be on his side, show him you're on his side and he'll talk to you . . ."

She would try.

She heard him come home.

It was late afternoon.

He did not call out to her.

He did not look in on her.

He went to his room. She stayed in her room.

She slept.

On Saturday morning Maureen prepared a lavish breakfast, English style. Steve prowled and sniffed and said, "Uh boy." There were many platters. There was bacon, there was fried ham, there was oatmeal and sweet cream, and there was steak and sausages and kippers from a can and pancakes and syrup and poached eggs, and cups of black coffee with heavy whipped cream on top.

"Eat," Maureen said. "Eat up, oh lord and master. Gorge yourself. Me too."

They ate. They gorged themselves, and then at last they lay back in their chairs and sipped hot coffee through cold whipped cream.

"I wish to say something," Maureen said.

"Say," Steve said.

"I wish to ask something of you."

"Oh, this vixen." He licked whipped cream and sipped coffee. "She plies you with food—which is much more efficacious than plying with drink—and then, when you're at her mercy, she homes in for the kill. Speak to me; tell me what you wish to ask of me."

"Not really to ask. To tell. I want to tell you I believe in you. Whatever it was that happened to you up there in the attic, I believe you. I've been thinking about it, all of it. You hear a ringing that I don't hear—you hear that little red phone up there, a toy telephone, you hear it ringing—who the hell am I to say you don't hear it? I don't but you do."

First he frowned, then his forehead smoothed. He inclined his head, smiling a small smile. His expression was near beatific. "You're incredible," he said. "I used to know it, but all screwed up in my middle-aged problems, I lost it, I forgot you're the most wonderful human being that ever happened to me."

She poured more coffee for both of them and topped the coffee with dabs of whipped cream. "But I have a question, friend husband . . . A little red phone, a toy in the attic. It rings, but only you hear the ringing. You go up there and answer the ring and you're talking to Jack Mercer who is dead. He *is* dead, isn't he?"

"Is that your question?"

"No."

"Yes, Jack Mercer is dead. Eight years dead."

"Now my question: how do you explain it?"

She could see that he liked that question. The last of his reserve, the standoff crafty look in his eyes, disappeared. Now there was no barrier. The dark eyes were naked, vulnerable. "You're asking me what I've been asking myself. Am I crazy? Or is someone from what I believe is called the other side trying to communicate with me—"

"Other side? Jack? You believe that Jack is trying to communicate with you?"

"I know, I know . . . here I am, the world's number one rationalist, debunker of the supernatural, and yet . . . it's either that, or it's straitjacket time. Yes, friend wife, I do believe . . . I have to believe . . . that Jack Mercer is trying to communicate with me. Me. Steve Blair who doesn't believe in astrology, cosmology, spiritualism, life after death, reincarnation, *none* of it. Me, Steven Blair, who doesn't even believe for sure in God. But here I am trapped in a syllogism. I am either conked-out, all-out, straitjacket crazy—or there *is* life after death and Jack Mercer is reaching through and trying to get to me. Either I'm nuts and I have to be put away—or there's something doing out there. Can you imagine?"

"No, not really—"

"Nor could I—before this. Toy phones don't ring. If they do, the sound of that ringing should not be restricted to me. And when I go to answer, it's impossible that the faint voice straining to get through is the voice of a man long dead, our dear friend Jack Mercer. But if all of that is *not* true—

than I really have to be carted off to the bughouse. I don't . . . didn't . . . believe in God, but I remember a quote . . . 'God moves in a mysterious way His wonders to perform.'" He drank coffee, wiped whipped cream from his lips. "Okay. It's either the booby hatch or I believe and honest to God I *do* believe. But what? That the dead are trying to talk to me? How crazy can you get? Can *I* get?"

"Do you think you're crazy?"

"No."

"Heart and soul?"

"I don't think I'm crazy—from all the way down to the boots of my soul. I think I *sound* crazy and I think you may *think* I'm crazy . . ."

She got up and went round to him and kissed the back of his head over his ear. "Count me in," she said. "Whatever the hell is going down here, don't exclude me. I don't think you're crazy, there'll be the two of us, and together we'll be able to *prove* that you're not crazy."

He leaned back, looked up to her.

"I love you," he said.

"I love you," she said.

She had to believe that too.

It was a honeymoon weekend, Steve and Maureen Blair alone, no children, nobody. The sun was hot, the sky was blue, the sea was cool, and the surf in their cove was brash and foamy. On Saturday they picnicked on the white sand, listened to opera on the portable radio and swam naked in the sea. On Sunday, compliment of compliments, he took her fishing with him. In the evening she cooked the fish and made French fries and opened a bottle of white wine. They were a married couple, they could not be closer, they adored each other, but without sex. She loved him, but had to admit she was not in love with him, and she felt guilt, this married woman, because she was *in* love with someone else.

They had a close warm lovely weekend: a honeymoon.

And in the attic the little red phone did not ring.

Eight ∼∞∞∞

DR. SAM'S diagnosis (and tentative prognosis) had hit the mark. The aural hallucinations had indeed been the crisis. There were no more hallucinations, no more ringing phone, and the depression had begun to wane. July went by, and it was August, and Steve was wonderful, no longer gaunt, not hollow-eyed, and his mood was up, it was cheerful, it was in fact ebullient, perhaps *because* the little red phone had finally ceased to ring. He looked great, chocolate brown from the sun, his skin glowing, his eyes bright. He jogged five miles a day. In his study he read his books feet up on the table. In the backyard, he played baseball with his family. He never failed to accompany them to the cove for swimming, and he went off regularly with Josh for fishing. Her calls to Dr. Sam—from Alan Harrison's house—were optimistic.

"Good, good," Dr. Sam Vaughn had exulted and then, at last, late in August, he had posed the inevitable question. "How're we doing on the connubial situation?"

"Nothing," she said.

"Make that nothing yet." He laughed. "From what you've been telling me, dear Maureen, I can tell you, pretty soon it *will* happen. And then we'll be all well, all recovered, won't we?"

Will we? she thought. She was silent.

"Maureen . . ."

"I'm right here."

And when she hung up she thought again, Will we? What

you don't know, doc—there's a new sickness growing here, and it's me. She wondered what would happen if it *did* happen as Dr. Samuel Vaughn so sanguinely predicted. Would she deny him? Would she deny her husband? She knew she would not. She was the wife, he was the husband, and they were sworn—but he would know. Steven Blair, sensitive Steve would know she was accepting him dutifully as a wife but not responding. He would know she was no longer in love with him that way. What he would not know, *could* not know, was that she was in love with another man that way and every other way. But she did not sleep with that one either: because she was Maureen Kirby Blair.

She did, though, see him whenever she took the kids into town: they would meet in their little park and on those days, if everything fell into place, they would drive out to Clare Selwyn's for lunch. But on Saturdays, regularly, they *always* went to lunch at Clare Selwyn's Inn—at a sacrifice to everybody, including Clare. Sacrifice to Maureen: she gave up the pleasure of her children on Saturdays. Saturday was her shopping day and she insisted that the shopping was *her* chore and no one else's: she drove into town alone. Sacrifice to Dr. Alan Harrison: he had to juggle his office appointments so that he was fully free on Saturday until three. But the real sacrifice was Clare's—because on Saturdays her restaurant was closed to customers.

"Even the Lord had one day of rest," Clare would say in justification. On Saturdays her staff was off: her staff was two waitresses. And on Saturdays her lodgers would have to fend for themselves. Her permanent lodgers were three— two old women and one old man—and they enjoyed their Saturdays, cooking for themselves and cleaning the dishes and sometimes cooking for Clare. On Saturdays Clare Selwyn would stay in bed until eleven o'clock and—before Dr. Alan and Mrs. Blair—sometimes even until noon, which was virtually hedonistic in the township of Acheron Falls in the great state of Maine.

But with the advent of Mrs. Maureen Blair, Clare Selwyn's Saturday habits began to change. The old woman recognized that the relationship between Dr. Alan and Mrs. Blair was a romance, albeit more innocent than Clare presumed. And so one weekday after lunch, she took Harrison aside.

"I been lookin' at you two people and what I been seein' shoots off sparks. I don't know what's goin' on between you two, but I like what I see because I am an old busybody from way back. So you listen to Auntie Clare, young fella. I want you and your lady to come here every Saturday, like a regular date, you know, a rendezvous. Ain't nobody out here on Saturday, I am closed. Ain't nobody here except my old lodgers, and they's too old to know nuthin' from anything at all, if you know what I mean. So you and your lady comes out on Saturdays for lunch at twelve o'clock, which I will personal cook up for you and serve you while the weather holds up at your table out there under the tree. And when the weather turns, I have a cozy little corner inside by the fireplace . . ."

They had met in June, it was now late August, and they knew what was going on between them. They were in love but it remained unspoken; they declared it by gesture, signal, body language, the touch of hands. She knew he wanted her, and he knew she wanted him, but they knew it could not happen, not to them. She was a young woman, but a woman steeped in old-fashioned tenets; she was a modern woman but her roots were in her early-training Catholicism. And he, not religious but the scion of religious parents, understood her and respected her feelings.

In their talks, without deep confidences, they learned about their lives before they met and about their lives now. She told him in nebulous outline, without really breaching confidence, about Steve's illness, his depression, his impotence and her resultant celibacy; and he told her about his devastation at the death of his wife, and *his* celibacy since that death. Yes, he was a modern relatively young man with

91

some deeply ingrained old-fashioned principles. Only the state of Maine, he guessed, could grow the likes of him . . . But his eyes told her that he was now in love.

One day she said bluntly: "In all my years of marriage, I've never cheated, and to cheat now on a man who is sick, a man who loves me, would be, for me, impossible. I just could not live with myself. But I can promise you this, Alan. When he's better—when he's for sure all better—I can talk to him about divorce, and I will. I'm certain he'll understand. He's a good man, unselfish, compassionate . . ."

School started the day after Labor Day and then every weekday she drove the kids to school and picked them up after school, and one day, a Monday, when she came home after delivering the kids, she called to Steve and there was no reply, and she knew where he was.

She ran up quickly, opened the attic door.

He was seated on the floor, his legs crossed Indian fashion, the little red phone in his lap, the receiver to his ear. He looked at her as though he did not see her. "Maureen," he said. He was frowning, the receiver pressed to his ear. His mouth was tight; he was straining to hear. "No good." He moaned. "It's no good."

"What?" she whispered. "What's no good?"

The frown spread over his face.

"I hear him, it's him, it's his voice, but it's so far away, too faint, it's too faint. He just can't get *through*." There were tears in his eyes. "He wants to tell me something. Maureen, he wants to *tell* me something. But it gets fainter and fainter, each time fainter. Soon—I know it—it'll go away entirely . . ."

He slapped down the receiver. He stood up, faltered, then carried the little phone to its shelf. He put it away and then he stumbled to her, extended his arms and embraced her. She could feel his weight, and she knew. Steven Blair—the strong man no longer strong, the irreligious man now religious, the skeptic now astonished—was leaning on her for support, he was clinging to her, but she was an abstraction, a symbol. *He was clinging to his sanity.*

"It's not as bad as you think," said Dr. Sam Vaughn over the telephone. "Actually, there's some very good news in what you've told me."

"Didn't you *hear* me? It's started all over again! The ringing! That damned little red phone—"

"Aside from that—how is he?"

"Why are you changing the subject?"

"I'm not."

"You are!"

"Maureen, please get hold of yourself. Please answer me. How is he otherwise?"

"*Otherwise*, he's okay, but—"

"Maureen, do you think he's crazy?"

"I—I don't know."

"Do you want me to come out there?" She could tell from his voice that he knew what her reply would be. "Do you want me to arrange for his hospitalization?"

"No . . ."

"Then let me tell you, and I know it'll help—you do *not* think he's crazy. And I agree. There are many people who are quite sane but are afflicted by a single, harmless aberration. In Steve's case, at the tail end of a depression, he's come up with a toy telephone that only rings for him. And when he answers, he has Jack Mercer trying to talk to him from the great beyond. But Jack never does get to talk to him, does he? There's never an up-and-back conversation, is there? And best of all, Jack's voice is getting fainter and fainter. Your quote—Steve's quote—is most encouraging: 'But it gets fainter and fainter, each time fainter; soon—I know it—it'll go away entirely . . .' You couldn't have given me better tidings, Maureen. There we have Steve's unconscious coming through, we have his psyche telling us that soon it'll go away entirely. *He's* telling us, soon it'll all disappear and he'll be out of it."

93

"I hope. Dear God, I hope."

She saw Dr. Alan Harrison almost every weekday—the kids coming out of school—in their park and earlier during the summer she had been seeing him without the kids every Saturday for their wonderful lunch at Clare Selwyn's, and now in early September they continued at Clare's. They were lovers, true lovers but without making love, which in a way proved themselves to themselves—she the staunchly reared Catholic and he the progeny of Calvinist stern New England parents. Maine parents.

He knew about Steve, the mid-life mental illness, but she still had not spoken about Steve's ringing phone. It would not be fair. She *wanted* to talk about it—it would relieve her to let it out with Alan—but it would make Steve sound so really crazy . . . and now Dr. Sam was convinced that the whole damn thing would truly pass, and soon.

So, for now, not fair. Only in the future, when Steve was better. Yes, the future . . .

On this second Saturday in September they drove out to Clare Selwyn's Inn, talking this day all the way about that wonderful old woman. They were aware that Clare regarded them as lovers and they laughed as they talked about the room that Clare had assigned to them "in order that you folks can rest up a mite after lunch." They used the room regularly so as not to disappoint the old woman who, only for them, romantically served a Saturday luncheon. It was a big sweet-smelling room with a plump double bed and a key prominently hanging from the lock on the inside. They went there after lunch every Saturday, and turned the key in the lock, and turned down the bed covers and even punched the pillows and lay on the bed.

It was close to cruel and unnatural punishment.

Unnatural.

How much longer could it go on?

The second Saturday in September, their table under

the tree was not set for lunch. It was bare, its chairs pushed up close under it. And there was no evidence of Clare Selwyn: no bustling, smiling, rosy-faced greeting. "You think she overslept?" Maureen asked.

"Let's go find out."

They went round to the rear where in the warm sunshine the lodgers were seated at a table, playing pinochle.

"Hey, Dr. Alan," said Perry Harding.

"Good afternoon, Perry. And a good afternoon to you, Rebecca, and to you, Anna."

"Afternoon," said Rebecca Page.

"Afternoon," said Anna Dickinson.

"I'm looking for Mrs. Selwyn."

"Ain't she about?" said Rebecca.

"Seems not," Harrison said.

"Probably takin' a long beauty sleep," Harding said. "You wan' me to go check her out, doc?"

"You set where you are and play pinochle," Anna said. "Dr. Alan's right capable of checkin' out by hisself. Ain't you, doc?"

"I am." Harrison took Maureen's arm and they went away from the pinochle game. "I don't like it," he said.

"Why?" His low tone frightened her.

"I'm the croaker."

"The what?"

"Vernacular in Maine for doctor. I'm the croaker and she's my patient and she's eighty-one years of age. When they're eighty-one and they don't show up where they're supposed to show up, and you're the croaker, you get worried."

"She *could* be oversleeping."

"Of course."

They went all the way around to the front door. It was unlocked. "No cause for alarm," Harrison said. "This is rural Maine, but even in *urban* Maine a great many people still leave their doors unlocked."

"That's the way it used to be in Bayfield County, Wisconsin."

Inside, Harrison called, "Clare!"

There were echoes but no answer.

At the bottom of the stairs he called loudly, "Clare!"

Again only echoing answers.

They climbed the stairs and he pointed at a closed door. Maureen hung back. He went forward, Maureen trailed behind. He opened the door and they went in.

"Clare," he said.

She was lying in the middle of her big bed. There was a pillow under her head and a pillow beside her. She was wearing a long nightgown with a short bathrobe over it.

She was rigid. Her lips were blue.

He touched her for a pulse. "She's gone," he said. "The old heart just gave out."

Maureen crossed herself.

Nine ~∞∞~

IT WAS the law that unexplained sudden death had to be reported to the police, and the law had it that any such unexplained or unattended death required a postmortem by the county officials. Alan Harrison made the call to the office of Chief Marcus Nolan, and then he and Maureen went down to the pinochle game to inform the lodgers.

"Oh my God," Perry Harding said.

Rebecca Page stared in disbelief.

Anna Dickinson said, "All right if we go up to see her?"

"I'm afraid not," Harrison said. "She wasn't sick, she wasn't being attended by a physician, and nobody was with her when she died. So it's a police matter, and nobody's allowed up there. We're waiting for Chief Nolan, and he is right now waiting for the county coroner—the medical examiner. They should be here within the hour."

They arrived in five separate official cars. There was Chief Nolan's car, the state troopers' car, the medical examiner's car, the medical examiner's photographer's car, and the hearse for the county morgue. And the five cars had hauled ten people: Chief Nolan and one of his policemen, two state troopers, the medical examiner and his stenographer, the photographer and his assistant. Five cars and ten people, Alan Harrison thought, and all for the natural death of one little old lady. That is the meaning (and the waste) of bureaucracy, he thought, but at least they worked swiftly.

First the photographer, assisted by his assistant, took

pictures, then turned the body over to the medical examiner. The medical examiner, before examining it, asked questions, and his stenographer took notes. The medical examiner ascertained that Dr. Alan J. Harrison and Mrs. Maureen Blair, who had come for lunch, had discovered the body.

"You did not permit any of the others to enter this room, did you, Dr. Harrison?"

"That's correct. I did not."

"You were Mrs. Selwyn's physician?"

"Yes. And also the physician for the lodgers. By the way, doctor, Mrs. Selwyn was eighty-one and she was the youngest of them."

"I take it you examined her when you found her?"

"A quick look."

"Your diagnosis?"

"Died in her sleep. Heart failure."

The medical examiner bent to the bed, did a cursory examination. "Yes, I think the autopsy will bear you out. You do know, Dr. Harrison, that in these cases an autopsy is mandatory."

"Yes."

The medical examiner smiled at the state troopers and said, "Thank you." The state troopers saluted and went away. At a gesture from the medical examiner, the driver of the hearse and his assistant enclosed Clare Selwyn in a canvas stretcher and carried her out.

"It's the law," the medical examiner said, "that the postmortem report is transmitted to the local police authority, who in this case is Chief Nolan. As to the body—when no next of kin has come forward—we're authorized to notify the physician of record. You are such, are you not, Dr. Harrison?"

"Yes."

"If we notify you, you will arrange to pick up the body?"

"Yes."

"Thank you."

The medical examiner smiled at his stenographer and she packed up and they departed and that left only Chief Nolan (and his policeman) and immediately the chief took over. Notebook in hand, he asked questions and wrote answers, and then one of his shotgun questions elicited a surprising response. The question, in general to everybody: "Did anything unusual happen here this morning?"

"Well, yeah," Perry Harding said.

The chief looked without enthusiasm at the old man. "What?"

"The phone rang."

"That's unusual?"

"Well, it was seven o'clock in the mornin'."

"Where were you?"

"In my room."

"And you heard the phone?"

"The way Miz Selwyn had it fixed, it rung real loud downstairs, and medium-soft upstairs in her room, which is the same connection."

"Real loud from downstairs—it woke you?"

"No, it ain't that loud, chief."

"Then what are you talkin' about?"

"I was up. I happened to be up. I got wakened up by a nightmare. I sat up, sweatin' bullets, looked at the clock. It was seven o'clock. I was just about to fall back to sleep when I hear the phone, and then Miz Selwyn answers it."

"Hold up, Perry."

"Yup, chief. I'm aholdin'."

"Okay, you hear the phone. Okay? Right?"

"Okay, yes, right. So what is that—?"

"Perry, how do you get the nerve to say, without your knowin', that Miz Selwyn answers the phone?"

"I got you there, chief. I am up because of the nightmare. I hear that phone down there. But it's three rings—only three rings. Nobody calls up and lets ring only three times. When it is three, then it's somebody pickin' up. Miz Selwyn she's a light sleeper, ask the girls here. The phone rings, and she picks up on the third, and when it is seven o'clock in the mornin', to me that is unusual."

Nolan looked to the ladies. "Light sleeper?"

"Yes," Rebecca said.

"Absolutely," Anna said.

"You ladies hear that phone, that seven o'clock phone?"

"No," the ladies said.

Harding said, "Me, I went back to sleep."

"And what time you wake up?"

"Nine-thirty."

"And you, Rebecca?"

"About the same. Nine-thirty."

"Anna?"

"Ten o'clock. Then we had breakfast, which always on Saturday we make ourself. Because like Perry told you— on Saturday Clare would stay late in bed for the old beauty sleep."

"Okay, I think I got all I need." The chief slapped away his notebook. He hooked his thumbs in his gun belt, frowned thoughtfully. "I'll have my wife come over. You all know Miz Nolan. She'll stay till we turn up some next of kin. I know there's a sister in Detroit, but after we check out Miz Selwyn's things, we should know a lot more. In the meantime my missus'll take care you folks."

Maureen drove home with her supermarket bags of shopping, and the problem posed by the sudden death of Clare Selwyn. Clare's death would be the talk of the town, but the town would also talk about Dr. Alan Harrison and Mrs. Maureen Blair and their every-Saturday lunches out at Clare Selwyn's Inn. Mrs. Marcus Nolan would get it from the three old well-meaning lodgers, and then Mrs. Marcus Nolan would spread it about the town like feed for chickens. The word was gossip. Small towns especially craved it. Well, forget the gossips. But Steve . . .

She would tell him quickly, and thus preempt the mouths

of Acheron Falls. Not that such mouths were of interest to Steven Blair, nor was he subject to them. He never went to town. Since their arrival in June he had only driven through the township of Acheron Falls, had never once stopped. But the avenues of gossip were devious, Maureen knew. A workman from town, coming out to the Blairs' house for some job, could mischievously let out the gossip at Steve by way of a pointed question . . .

She must preempt. She must tell him of her occasional Saturday lunches with Dr. Alan Harrison. That was the key word—occasional. There had been nobody out there with a calculator taking count: the old lodgers were far more interested in their pinochle than in Clare's Saturday lunches for Dr. Alan and his blond lady friend. Steve knew about Alan Harrison—from her, from Josh, from Laurie—and he had appreciated Harrison's help with the kids during the summer when they had sat for the board of education's aptitude tests. He knew about Diana Harrison and her friendship with Laura and with Josh, and he knew—from her, from Josh, from Laurie—that Dr. Harrison often met with them after school in the park. He certainly knew that Laurie spent weekends with Diana at Dr. Harrison's home. What he did not know—and would now know—was that on occasion, on a Saturday, Dr. Harrison would take Maureen to lunch to talk about the kids, the school, the guidance counselors, athletics, the drama society, the PTA . . .

Now as Maureen drove up the gravel roadway toward the garage she saw, to her right, Steve apparently digging up weeds on the lawn. He waved to her and she waved back. It was a warm September, the sun was hot. "Hold it," he called. She braked the car. "Just hold it right there," he called. She pulled up the emergency brake and turned off the ignition.

He trotted to her and leaned in through the rolled-down window. He looked old—too old. His eyes were haggard. "Where you been?" he said.

"Town. Shopping. What's the matter?"

"I want the car. I've been waiting a long time."

"Where the kids?"

"Backyard playing ball. Where you been so long?"

"Excitement in town. Poor old Clare Selwyn died in bed and we found her."

"Who? Who's Clare Selwyn and *who* found her?"

"Give me a hand with the shopping bags; there's a lot of them back there."

In the kitchen he helped distribute the contents of her packages. She said, "Clare Selwyn was a very old lady who owned Clare Selwyn's Inn a few miles out of town. Every now and then on a Saturday Dr. Harrison invited me there for lunch. We'd talk about Laurie, Diana, the kids, school, you know . . ."

"Yeah." He was not interested. She breathed more easily.

"We went there today. For lunch."

"So . . . ?"

"The old lady was nowhere about. We went up to her room. She was in bed. Dead—"

"Honey, I'm afraid I really don't care, I've got my own troubles, and they're monumental."

"Yes, darling," she said. "Yes, of course." She had done it. Preemption. The gossip was defused, it could no longer sneak up on him, surprise him . . . Poor Steve, he looked so tired. "Tell me," she said.

"It's been ringing all day, it's been driving me crazy. But there's almost nothing there on the other end. It's a voice, I know it's a voice, I know it's Jack's voice, but it's now so faint it's barely even a whisper, it's beyond a whisper, it's more like a gasp, a last desperate gasp . . ." He sat down. God, he looked so dreadfully tired.

"You said you wanted the car."

"Yes." He jumped to his feet. He smiled. But his face was so sad. "You know, my head really is going. I forgot . . . Maury, when I was with Josh in Jackson City buying chemicals . . . I went to a bookstore, bought some books.

Well, when I was there I came on a most interesting old tome, and then something diverted me and I put it back in its bin and that was that. Please remember, at that time the ringing had only just begun and I myself wasn't sure . . . Well, today it came back to me real strong and I think I even remembered the title . . . *The Arcane Brought Up To Date*. And the subtitle, something about the spirit world in modern times. From the moment I remembered, I've been waiting on pins and needles for you to get back with the car. I just hope that damn book is still there." He looked sheepish. "Here we go again . . . skeptic, wise guy non-believer, and look at me now, hell-bent to get going to Jackson City to find out if . . ." He took her face in his hands, kissed her forehead. "G'bye, honey."

The kids came in demanding food; they were always hungry. Not yet teenagers but already adolescents, they had grown and filled out over the summer, Josh far outstripping Laura. She was beautiful, he was handsome; their faces were smooth, innocent, similar of feature, with huge blue eyes and that wonderful crown of flaxen hair; identical twins, but he towered above her. Josh was already five feet eight and as brawny as he was tall, a powerful young man. God, he looks so much older than twelve, Maureen thought. Not the face, the body. Well, she thought, make that twelve years and five months . . .

And then at six o'clock they ate again, dinner, and Josh said, "You think dad ran off with another woman?"

"What would he want with another woman when he has mother?"

"Thank you, Laurie," Maureen said, feeling terrible.

Josh pointed at the kitchen clock. "Where is he?"

"I told you," Maureen said.

"It's after six," Josh said pointedly . . . snidely? . . . "Aren't you worried?"

"We're talking about your father Steven Blair, Josh. We're

talking about Steven Blair and Jackson City and a bookstore and books. You know about your father's fascination with books, I presume."

"Yes, I do."

"Are you worried?"

"No . . . I'm not."

"Good, then let's all settle down and not look for trouble where there's no reason . . ."

He returned at eight o'clock. Maureen heard the car grind into the garage; immediately she reported to the kids, who were watching television in the recreation room.

"Dad's home."

Josh only shrugged.

"He was the one who was worrying," Laura said.

"Mother talked me out of it, remember?"

"We were getting worried. It's late."

"What time?"

"It's after eight."

"I was reading."

"Hungry? I've been saving supper."

"Thanks, no."

"I'm not talking leftovers," Maureen said airily. "I'm talking hot food."

"I've eaten."

"Oh?"

He pulled a book from the pocket of his jacket. It had hard covers but it was the size of a paperback. "It was still there," he said. "I found it, I bought it. It explains a lot. Poppycock or no, believe or don't believe—for *us* it explains a lot. I stopped off in a restaurant in Jackson City, and I ate and started to read, and I read it all the way through. I've marked it for stuff to read to you. Are you interested?"

"Of course I'm interested." As per Doctor Sam.

The title was indeed *The Arcane Brought Up To Date*. The

subtitle was "The Spirit World In Modern Times." The author was a Neelam L. K. Braxton. "From the flyleaf we learn that he's a retired professor from Trinity College, Cambridge University." Steven sipped coffee. "I'll say in advance that I know that the English are notorious for their deep belief in ghosts, ectoplasm, haunted houses and pianos that play when there's no one in the room. Okay?"

"Please proceed."

"From the flyleaf we also learn that Professor Braxton is a student of the occult, but he takes no sides. His book is a compilation. It takes in, and breaks down, worldwide data, and the reader may believe or not believe as he or she sees fit."

"But, will you also say in advance that you are aware that professors—Yale, Harvard, Cambridge, Oxford—can be as kooky or kookier than the kookiest of their students?"

"Yes, I certainly do."

"Okay, go."

He opened the book. "I'll now read a few of the passages that I marked off. When we're finished I'll give you the book for you to read if you like."

. . . there are writings, from time immemorial, that report communications between those who are living and those who have passed over . . . Steven turned pages. *. . . Sir Oliver Lodge, 1851–1940, a scientist, a famous physicist, not only professed his belief in the possibility of communication between the living and the dead, but finally, and in full knowledge of the furor it would engender, he published an account of his conversations with his dead son Raymond . . .* "Now listen to this. . . . *the communications were effected by means of psychics, trance mediums, or other such specially gifted persons, but in the latter half of the twentieth century the phenomena began to occur without the nexus of another person, without a go-between; in fact without the desire of the living person to communicate with the dead. The phenomena occurred spontaneously and the means was undramatic: the mundane telephone. A phone would ring, a person would answer and the voice that came through was the voice of someone who had passed over. In*

the field of the occult there are all too often pronouncements from persons of unsound mind. But such reports began to come in from all over the world, and they were collated, and in time they meshed to a body of knowledge which, if it could not be explained, could not be denied; to wit: certain of the dead communicate with certain of the living and the means of the communication is the telephone.

. . . there are disputes among the researchers—who calls to whom and why—but on one point the researchers are agreed, because the overall data are the same all over the world: the voice of the recent dead comes through loud and clear; the voice of the less recent dead comes through less loud and clear; and within a few years of the time of death the voice is faint and continues to grow fainter and, no matter the tenacious efforts of the one who has passed, his voice fades and continues to fade until there is no voice on the other end, until there is nothing on the other end but silence, dead silence . . .

Steven snapped the book shut.

It was a shot. Maureen jumped.

"What do you think?" he said.

"It's eerie, scary—"

"Not the point. Point is—do you *believe* it can be? Point is—do you now believe *me*? That it was Jack Mercer on the phone? Do you believe it's possible that a dead man, long dead, was trying to get through, *did* get through to the other side, to me?"

She fought him, she had to fight to keep her sanity. Sorry, Doctor Sam. "You read to me about telephones. You didn't read about *toy* telephones. Is there anything in that book about toy telephones?"

He poured coffee, drank, put down the cup and grinned. It was terrible, not a grin but a rictus. And for a moment he not only looked tired . . . he looked dead. "It's cold up here," she said to cover. "Aren't you cold?"

"It's not cold, Maury. It's you. What I read to you. It's made you cold."

He poured coffee into her cup. She drank it gratefully.

"I thought about that too," he said.

"What?"

"Toys. Toy telephones."

"Good."

He grinned again. She could not look. She turned her head. "Let's try to be logical," he said.

"Yes," she said, oh God, please, yes . . .

"We'll play devil's advocate and try to be logical about the illogical."

"Sure."

"There they are out there, the sincere scientists in the world of the crazies, like, back there in time, Sir Oliver Lodge, and like right here in time, Professor Neelam L. K. Braxton. Okay?"

"Okay." She wanted to scream.

"There's some kind of consensus among them, the believers, the *scientific* believers, that in this latter half of the twentieth century dead people—over there in the great beyond—have been communicating with live people, right here in this beyond, by means of—go believe it—the telephone. Alexander Graham Bell. How crazy can you get? Involving AT&T in the occult. If it ever gets out can you imagine what would happen to the stock market? Can you imagine? Talk to me, Maury."

"Yes, I can imagine."

"Thank you for talking to me."

"Please. Not now, don't get testy."

"Right. Forgive me. Where was I?"

"Alexander Graham Bell. AT&T. The stock market."

"The occult," he said. "Logical about the illogical. Okay. If the dead can talk—and they can talk to you through the Bell telephone—why can't they talk to you through a toy telephone? In what you call the eerie, and I call the craziness and they call the occult—can you perceive any difference? If by the Bell telephone, why not a toy telephone? How am I doing?"

"Just fine." Oh lord, he really was crazy . . .

"But what's important to us, and fits with us, is the business of no communication, the business of Jack's voice, very faint, that keeps dying and dying away until now it's just nothing. In some crazy way that's our proof. I told it to you before I read it to you. I told it to you before I knew that the scientists knew about it. I told it to you before I read to you from Professor Neelam L. K. Braxton."

"Yes, Steven, you certainly did."

"I'm going to do it again. I'm going to read it to you once more, just that one passage about the voice of the recent dead coming through loud and clear, and the voice of the less recent dead less loud and clear, and in a few years of the time of death the voice growing fainter and no matter the efforts of the one who has passed, his voice fading until there's no voice on the other end, until there's nothing on the other end but silence, dead silence . . ."

Would this, she wondered, ever stop?

Ten ∞

ON MONDAY, after dropping the kids at school, she made the call from Alan's house and informed Dr. Samuel Vaughn of the new turn of events. She told him about Steve's remembering some book he'd browsed through in a bookstore in Jackson City, of his quick trip on Saturday and his return with the damn thing. And she told him about their talk Saturday night and of shorter talks on the same subject yesterday.

Dr. Sam was not disturbed. To the contrary. "Maureen, I'm now going to do what I dislike doing. I'm going to talk psychiatric talk to a layman."

She could hear his sigh at the other end of the wire.

"He's going to come out of it, Maureen. He's preparing you and himself. He's setting the stage, however unconsciously. He is going all the way back to a book he happened to look through . . . when was it?"

"June."

"At the beginning of the ringing phone?"

"Yes."

"And now he's back to it. Now he remembers it. It's another nonsense book, another of the sheer-nonsense occult books—a couple of years ago Steve Blair would have picked it apart and shown it up to be what they are all—ridiculous. But now he remembers. Now three months later he remembers, and he goes out and picks it up and brings it home as a deception for you, and a self-deception for him. Steve has selected from the book the alleged phenomenon of tel-

ephonic communication between the living and the dead—
and I hope you're aware that that is *not* what he has stressed.
He has stressed the discontinuance of such alleged communication. What he has stressed—ostensibly as his point
of proof—is that Jack Mercer came in faint, and is fading
off to fainter and is now finally drifting off for good and
all. I believe Steve's unconscious is setting the stage for Jack
to drift off permanently, and then Steven will be rid of his
demons, and the little red phone will be a child's toy
again . . ."

At two-fifteen in their little park in the warm September
sunshine, Alan Harrison sat with her on their favorite bench,
and they chatted about nothing; and then when school was
out, two-thirty, the kids—Diana and Josh and Laura—joined
them, and they were also joined by Chief Marcus Nolan.
"Got some news. Miz Selwyn's sister and her husband is
flyin' in from Detroit to take over out there at the inn as
next of kin. Ain't no other. There was a brother out by
California, but he got hisself a stroke last year and passed."
      "What do you hear from the county?" Harrison asked.
      "You are premature, doc. We have got to give them their
full time of work. I will let you know as soon as they pass
me the word, which should be the end of the week. And
you too, Mrs. Blair. After all, ma'am, you are entitled. I
mean you was right there when the corpse was discovered,
right?"
      If he says another word I'll kill him, Maureen thought.

On Thursday afternoon Maureen Blair, having driven the
kids home, lay in bed, in bra and panties, forcing herself
to read *The Arcane Brought Up To Date*. Suddenly she was
caught by an impulse to go up there to that damned little
red phone, to look at it, touch it, examine it. She was home
alone: the kids were at the cove and Steve was out jogging.
      Barefoot she went up the stairs to the attic. She opened
the door, left it open and walked slowly to the shelf with
110

the little red phone. She reached out for it but could not reach it. Her hands would not move, fear had incapacitated her. She tried, she struggled and then she stopped struggling. She let herself go loose. She opened her mouth and breathed deeply, scaring herself with the snuffling sounds coming from her throat. She closed her mouth, shutting off the noise. She breathed through her nose, almost choking—and then release. She was able to move. She took the little red phone from its shelf, holding it as if it were a fragile precious object of art.

A little red phone, a sturdy expensive toy, none the worse for its years; a right-angle metal crank extended from its side. She turned the crank: it produced a surprisingly loud reverberating ring. This was it? This ridiculous little instrument, a toy telephone, was the source, the provenance, of all their ills in Acheron Falls. I'll kill it, she thought, I'll smash it and we'll be done with this whole damned unholy charade. She laughed, a celebration. She held the little red phone over her head and was about to throw it against a wall—when she sensed someone in the room.

Someone—something—was next to her.

As she turned, the phone was wrested from her; a fist hit her in the mouth. She fell and was struck again, the back of her head to the floor. For moments she lay like that, as though in bed in a dream; then painfully, slowly, she turned and squirmed to her knees and remained in that posture, as if in genuflection, looking up.

Steve.

Steve in jogging suit and rubber-soled running shoes. With the little red phone in both hands held to his chest. Again that smile of the dead. She saw a dead man.

"Don't ever dare touch that again." His voice was dry, a notch above a whisper. "Don't you ever dare."

He restored the toy telephone to its place on the shelf. He turned and came back, and winced. Because now he saw *her*. He made a sound, a gasp. He reached down and helped her to her feet, and then his face seemed to dissolve and there were tears in his eyes, and she knew she had to try to help him . . .

When she went to bed she could not sleep, turning from side to side, finally lying flat on her back. Guilt. Twice now he had looked dead to her. Was she imagining what she wanted to see? She was in love with another man. The obstacle was her husband. As Dr. Sam might say, did she unconsciously want him out of the way?

She got out of bed. She sat by the window. She went to the bathroom cabinet, swallowed two sleeping pills, and then another. She plumped the bed, freshening it, fixed the pillows and lay on her back again, the sheet to her chin, waiting for sleep, and when it came a dream came with it, a kind of terrible punishment? She dreamed that *Josh* was in the bedroom. She dreamed that Josh, naked, got into bed with her. She dreamed that Josh, sweet, strong, innocent Josh, forced her thighs apart and entered her—twelve-year-old Joshua Mercer Blair was having intercourse with her? She tried to fight out of her dream, but could not. She struggled with all her strength to fight out of that obscene nightmare, but she could not. . . .

When she woke up the sun was shining. She was still on her back, legs apart. She was covered with perspiration. She actually felt pain, an ache in her lower parts. She shook her head, got out of bed and lurched to the shower, and as she stood there under the pounding stream of hot water she remembered her dream in every detail.

On this Friday morning Laura's alarm woke her fifteen minutes earlier than usual because, aside from packing the school stuff, she had to pack a bag; she would be staying with Diana for the weekend, all the way through until Monday, including Monday-morning school.

Her bag packed, Laura went across to the other end—to the north end over the garage—to Josh's room to help her mother wake him. Josh would not be staying this weekend with the Harrisons. "Weather's too nice to waste," he had said. "Dad and I have a lot of fishing to do."

They got Josh up—once he was in the shower he was officially up—and then Laura went down to the kitchen to help her mother with the breakfast. These days her dad rarely joined them. These days he slept late and skipped breakfast.

Also on this Friday, on the phone in Alan's house, Maureen experienced an unexpected reaction from Dr. Samuel Vaughn. For once he sounded concerned—for her.

"I don't like it," he said. "I don't like it at all."

"What not?" She said. "What don't you like? That I invaded his attic? That I dared examine that damned little phone? That I wanted to smash it against the wall? Or that stupidly I picked the wrong time to go up there and invade—"

"That he struck you."

"Oh?" she said.

"That's not good, Maureen. Until now, from all you've told me, I've been optimistic, even progressively optimistic. But now I'm afraid we've hit a snag, and a bad one. Violence. That's not like Steve. That's a bad turn, a basic shift in the personality pattern. And once it starts it can become dangerous. He never struck you before, did he?"

"No."

"Would you like to come back to New York, you and the children?"

He *was* concerned. "Doc, they're going to school here. We just can't keep pulling them up and transplanting them."

"All right," he said. "Perhaps I'll come up there. You won't tell him why, of course. I'll call and invite myself. I'll be coming for a visit."

"Doc . . ."

"Once I'm there, I'll arrange to have him hospitalized for a time."

113

"Doc, please . . ."

"Maureen, I repeat. When aberrant behavior shifts to violence—especially in a person whose patterns have never been violent—then such behavior can—repeat *can*—become dangerous."

"But not must?"

"No . . ."

"Then let's give him a chance. I wouldn't want, *ever*, to put him away, unless absolutely necessary and no alternative. It's Steve, doc. I'm upset too. Afraid. But I don't want to be responsible for—"

"He struck you. I was optimistic before, Maureen. I was honest with you then and I'm being honest with you now. We have to look at the bad side. It's not only you we have to worry about. The children . . ."

"God, he loves them."

"He loves you too."

"Not the way he loves those kids. He would never harm them, I'd stake my life on that . . ."

"What do you want to do, Maureen? You have an alternative suggestion?"

"Me. I will keep an eye on him, I will watch very very closely for any more changes. After all, I am the target, I'm putting *me* on the line. I'll call you every day, if necessary from home. If I see anything, sense anything, I'll call you immediately."

He was not convinced, but in this case, as in too many in his profession, the doctor did not have all the answers. His less than accurate earlier prognosis was proof of that. So, reluctantly, he agreed, reminding her he would be there instantly if there was any further incident.

"I love you, Doctor Sam."

"Be careful, Maureen."

She came early to their park bench, but he was already there. She sat near him, said nothing. At length she said, "How do I look?"

114

"A bit peaked, would be my learned diagnosis."

"Been having some stormy sessions at home. But that's not it."

"What is—it?"

"A bad dream last night."

"Want to talk about it?"

"No." But of course she did, and could not. Thank God he was so patient with her . . .

He looked past her. "School's out," he said.

The kids came romping, shouted their greetings, circled their parents, sat in the grass directly behind the bench.

And then Chief Marcus Nolan, Stetson poised on the middle of his head, his tightly cinched gun belt bifurcating the huge bulge of his belly, was marching toward them, a red portfolio tucked under his right arm. "Howdy," was his inevitable greeting.

Harrison said, "What brings you here, chief?"

"I got news and it's all bad. I got homicide on poor old Miz Selwyn. And I also got rape—"

"The hell you say."

"Just a minute," Maureen gestured over her shoulder toward the children in the grass.

"No, no minutes," Nolan said. "They ain't no babies need no pacifier. They're grown up enough to hear all this— for their own protection."

"All right, go on, chief," Harrison said. "What have you got?"

"The report from the coroner. The results of the postmortem, the autopsy; and all the photographs appertaining thereto."

"Appertaining thereto?" Harrison snapped. "Stop it, Marcus. You don't have anybody to impress here."

Nolan opened the red portfolio. "This here's for you, doc. It's a copy of the autopsy report to be given to the personal physician of the deceased. I am hereby givin' it to you, in the presence of a witness, Miz Maureen Blair. You don't have to read it all now. Turn them pages, please. Yeah. Right. Okay, now. This is it. Summation." Nolan tapped a thick finger on the typewritten page. "I know it by heart. 'The postmortem discloses beyond any scintilla of doubt that the deceased, Mrs. Clare Lowell Selwyn, was first raped and then put to death by means of suffocation.' "

Maureen was crying. The children were on their knees, looking up, behind the park bench.

Chief Nolan reached into the portfolio. "These here are the pictures, Alan. Now we understand a hell of a lot more than before. Look here on this one." The pudgy finger pointed. "The old lady is wearin' a bathrobe. There's the nightgown stickin' out on bottom and over the nightgown is the bathrobe. Who goes to sleep in a bathrobe? Nobody, is who. But I didn't pay that no never-mind and neither did you. Did you, doc?"

"No."

Nolan shuffled photographs. "Now look at this one. There's a pillow under her head, but there's this other pillow down there, pretty much scrunched up, by her side, like by the midsection. We didn't give that no never-mind either, did we? I mean who sleeps in a bathrobe? And also with a pillow out there by the midsection?"

The chief returned the photographs to the portfolio. "We got rape and murder, and the county officials have got it figgered out and I agree with them. They is somethin' on which we don't agree—but I will come to that . . . Perry told us that the phone rung at seven o'clock in the mornin'. Clare answered it. It was someone she knew and that someone said he wanted to come see her. She puts on her bathrobe and goes down and waits and lets him in. They go upstairs, to talk or somethin'. He closes the door, throws her on the bed, does her, then puts a pillow over her face till she suffocates. He throws the pillow aside, goes downstairs and out of the house."

Maureen glanced toward the children. They were still on their knees in the grass, heads tilted up, listening. She wondered if she should stop this? Herd them together and get them away? Or was the chief right? Were they old

116

enough to listen and learn and gain knowledge for their own protection? Were they old enough? Alan seemed to think so. He could have sent them off but hadn't.

". . . no sign of forced entry," Chief Nolan was saying, "so it had to be somebody she knew. We all agreed."

"What did you disagree about?" Harrison said.

"Mitch Ranson."

"Oh, no—"

"Oh yes. If it was Mitch who called, she figgered to let him in, crazy or no crazy. She was a feisty old woman, she wouldn't be afraid. Hell, she knew him, just like you, since he was a kid. Maybe he said he was hungry—"

"And maybe you're jumping at conclusions."

"That's what the county people say and they even say they got proof. There's been people out there dustin' for fingerprints and they got a whole load, and none of them fingerprints is Mitch's, which are on record. But they also got a whole load of smudges. Fingerprints is only easy on the TV. It has to be a crazy. It wasn't some kinda burglar. He didn't steal nuthin'. What he done was rape a woman eighty-one years old, which you gotta be crazy to do in the first place, and then he kills her with the pillow so's she can never identify him. It figgers Mitch—"

"*Why?*"

"He's the only crazy loose hereabouts."

"There are many crazies, chief, that we don't know are crazy. As for Mitch, who says he's loose hereabouts?"

"There've been rumors—"

"You checked those rumors?"

"I did."

"And what did you get?"

"I got nuthin', but that don't mean there ain't somethin'. You gotta go with the hunches, doc. I been in this business since I was knee-high to a tadpole and I learned a long way back that when you got a hunch goin' for you—I mean a real hard gut-type hunch—them kinda hunches very seldom send you up the creek."

117

"Seldom is not always."

"You said that very nice, doc. Maybe you want to impress Miz Blair—"

"I'm trying to stop you from making a fool of yourself."

"Well, thanks kindly, Dr. Harrison, but I would suggest that you stick to doctorin' and you let me stick to my business. I would appreciate, when you have the time, that you drop into the station house so's you and me can go over the medical examiner's report. That *is* your area."

On Saturday, lunch at Essie's house that Alan had invited Maureen to was sumptuous, and Maureen regretted Josh's absence. He loved food, he was, in fact, an enormous eater, and he would have consumed Essie's pungent roast loin of pork, her fried potato balls, her mushrooms in cheese sauce and her creamed broccoli.

Josh . . .

When they'd come home from school on Friday, minus Laura, Josh had regaled his father with the sensational news of Clare Selwyn's rape and murder and of Chief Marcus Nolan's hunch about an escaped lunatic named Mitchell Ranson. Steve had looked at Maureen, and she had answered, "Dr. Harrison and I happened to be in the park waiting for the kids to come from school. They came out and spread themselves in the grass behind us. When Chief Nolan appeared and told us about what happened to that poor old woman—"

"Tell him about the crazy," Josh had said. It came out like an order.

Maureen had told about Mitch Ranson, and there was a brief discussion, and then she saw Steve's eyes go away . . . he was no longer with them. "Anybody call?" she had asked.

"Not a single phone call," he said. . . .

And now at lunch on Saturday she emptied her mind and filled her stomach with Essie's succulent roast pork, as did Alan and even the girls.

Driving home, she felt bloated and sleepy.

The car safely parked in the garage, she was pleased to discover that she was home alone. There was a note on the refrigerator:

Maury: Gone fishing. Josh and I are out at the cove. We should be home about five o'clock. The phone did not ring, nobody called. See you later. Your obedient servant, Steven.

Gone fishing. How blessedly *normal.*
The phone did not ring. Better and better.
She locked the doors, climbed upstairs, kicked out of her shoes, plopped on the bed and almost at once was asleep.

She heard knocking.
Dimly, she heard the knocking.
It woke her. Somebody was banging on the door.
She looked at the clock: it was quarter to four. They were home early, but why were they knocking? Steve had keys. Had he forgotten his keys? Then she heard Josh.
"Mom! Open up! Mother! Are you home? Open *up!*"
She ran down.
She opened the door.
Josh was there alone.
He was covered with blood.

Eleven ∼∞∞∼

SHE COULD not even scream. She pulled him into the house, tore at his shirt. "Where? What happened to you—?"

"Not me." He was out of breath, he was panting.

"Where are you hurt?"

"I'm not hurt."

"You're all bloody, for God's sake."

"It's dad."

"Oh my God. Where is he?" She ran out the door. "Where?" She looked at Josh. *"Where?"*

"Let's get the car, mom."

"Where is he?"

"The cove."

She ran to the garage. She was not wearing shoes. She got into the station wagon, Josh beside her, and they roared out. "I ran all the way," Josh said.

"What happened? *Tell me.*"

"Fishing off the rocks . . . dad was on one side of the horseshoe, me on the other, my back to him. All of a sudden I hear him yell out, loud. I turn and I see them, dad going down and this guy with a rock in his hand banging at dad's head. I threw down my fishing pole and started hollering and running but it's a long way across the beach from one jetty to the other. I saw the guy pick up dad's fishing knife and bend toward him . . ."

Maureen was sobbing, not wanting to hear, having to hear . . .

"The guy dropped the knife and ran. But I know who he is."

"Dad? What about *dad*?"

"That's all I cared about, I didn't run after the guy . . . all I cared about was dad—"

"A good thing you didn't run after—"

"Dad was in real bad shape. His head was bashed, his throat was cut and the blood was coming out of him . . . there wasn't much I could do. I held him in my lap, I just held him, like trying to talk to him but he couldn't answer me . . ."

It was a five-minute drive. They left the car on the road, a dirt road, and ran to the cove, Josh pointing, along the north ridge of its U-shaped perimeter.

Steve was lying on his back, his open eyes glinting in the sunshine. His head was battered, white splinters of bone exposed. His throat was cut. A bloody knife, its handle wrapped in a fishing rag, was lying near him. Maureen, as though impelled, stooped to him to touch him. He was cold, lifeless cold. She stood up, clenched her hands, turned her face to the sky and, finally, screamed. She kept it up until she felt Josh's hands on her, one of his hands cupping her mouth.

She stopped then. She put her arms around her strong stalwart son, leaning on him for support while she quietly wept; then she used one of the clean fishing rags to wipe her face. "All right," she said, taking a deep breath. "We have to call the police. I hate to leave him here like this—"

"We can carry him to the car."

"No . . . that would be wrong to do." She shuddered. She kissed Josh's forehead. "The nearest phone is the one at home—but I don't want to leave him alone. Will you stay with him, Josh?"

"Sure."

"I'll be back real quick. I promise."

"I know you will, mom."

121

She kissed him again, turned and headed for the car.

As she drove off, her brave, stalwart Josh allowed himself to smile.

She left the car outside. She ran into the house and to the bar. She poured gin, gulped it. She called Acheron Falls, got through to Chief Marcus Nolan and told him, and told him she would wait for him at the cove and told him where their cove was. She called Alan, and told him. She went upstairs and put on her shoes, then somehow made it downstairs, outside, and ran to the car.

She sat on a wide flat rock with Josh. The sun in the west was still warm. "They'll be here soon, Chief Nolan and his officers. I called Dr. Harrison. He'll be here too. He said he's going to bring your sister. I tried to say no, to spare her, but he said it had to be sooner or later. I don't know . . . oh God, I don't know anything . . ."

Josh put his arm around his mother, consoling her.

She blew her nose on a clean fishing rag Josh somehow produced, then pulled at it until it tore. "About the man who . . . who . . . did this to dad. You said you knew him . . . ?"

"I think I recognized him—"

"Who?"

"Remember when Chief Nolan unrolled a kind of poster-picture and tacked it up on the wall in his office?"

"Yes."

"That's the man."

Six motor vehicles were lined up in the dirt road behind Maureen's station wagon—two police cars, a hearse from the funeral parlor in Acheron Falls, a photographer's car, Dr. Alan Harrison's car and a motorcycle belonging to a reporter from the town newspaper. They went about their respective tasks, and eventually Steve's body was taken off by the hearse.

122

Laura, sadistically in Maureen's view, was asked to identify her father's body, which she did dry-eyed and then
threw up.

"I think we ought to go back to the house now," Nolan
said. The chief had a great sense of the fitness of things,
Alan thought disgustedly.

Immediately after they entered the house Nolan said,
"No gates on the windows? Didn't anybody tell you, Miz
Blair? It ain't old times. We got a crime rate that keeps
soarin' without no letup, even in the great state of Maine.
Even without no crazy killer on the loose, you have gotta
have gates, Miz Blair. Now, tonight you and the kids will
spend the night in town. We will see to it that you are put
up right—"

"They'll stay at my house," Harrison said.

"All right. I'll leave one of my cops to be in charge here.
First off, when we get back to town I will want young Josh
here to look over that picture of Mitch Ranson and make a
positive identification. Doc, would you now go along with
me that it was Mitch done the old lady in?"

"In the light of these new developments—I think yes."

"Thankee, Dr. Harrison."

"Don't thank me. Thank this courageous young man, who
knows what he saw and I suspect will swear in court that
it was the man in the picture who did this awful thing—"

"I will," Josh said earnestly.

"Won't need no court of law," Nolan said. "Mitch's been
adjudged incurable insane. Once we grab him, he goes back
to the nuthouse and that'll be it. All we will need from this
young fella is his sworn statement and later on the positive
identification."

The poster-size picture of Mitchell Ranson was still
prominently displayed in the Acheron Falls police station.
Chief Nolan pointed. "Is that the man, young fella?"

"Yes," Josh said.

"You sure?"

"Absolutely."

"Okay, folks, this way." Nolan guided them into his office and arranged comfortable chairs for them: Maureen, Harrison, Laura. "But not you, not yet, young fella," he said to Josh.

Josh was clean and fresh in new clothes, his hair combed, his face shining. Back at the house he had stripped out of the bloody clothes, giving them to one of Chief Nolan's policemen. Then he had showered and dressed.

"You'll go with Officer Putnam," Nolan said. "He'll transcribe my questions and answers, then read them to you, and you'll swear them as your affidavit. Okay?"

"Yes, sir."

Josh marched out with Officer Putnam.

Nolan, in the swivel chair behind his desk, swung back to his guests. "Soon the county authorities will be here, Miz Blair. In matters of homicide the coroner's in charge, the medical examiner examines. It happens in this county the coroner and the medical examiner are one and the same. Also, the body of the deceased is not yet yours. In matters of homicide it is required that there be an autopsy. In this case I will special request that it be done promptly so's you can have the body back for whatever obsequies you may have in mind . . .

The county authorities worked quickly. It was put on the record that there were no fingerprints: nothing, of course, on the bloodstained rock, and only smudges, indecipherable, on the fishing rag wrapped around the hilt of the knife that had been the final weapon. The medical examiner did his duty with Steve's body—a rapid, perfunctory examination—and then in his capacity as coroner he promised the widow that the postmortem, mandatory, would be executed promptly and the body would be returned within the week to the funeral parlor in Acheron Falls.

Dr. Alan Harrison called on a single patient, necessary;

124

for all the rest Essie put through postponements. Then Dr. Harrison telephoned his friend Dr. Ronald Harvey.

"Ron, you're going to have to double up for me."

"Sure. For how long?"

"Seven to ten days."

"Starting when?"

"Now."

"You got it."

That's the way it always went between born Down Easters. No questions, each quick to oblige. Harrison informed Essie and then was free for at least a week to devote himself entirely to the bereaved Maureen Blair.

Maureen called Dr. Sam and when she told him, there was so long a silence on the other end that she almost hung up.

Finally he spoke. "Forgive me."

"Please, what's to forgive?"

"I'm crying, Maureen. A big piece of my personal world has fallen away. When Jack went—maybe because I was younger, more likely because I still had Steve—it didn't affect me like this—"

He stopped talking, but she heard him. His grief.

"I'll be out there early Monday morning," he said.

"We're staying with a Dr. Alan Harrison." She gave him the address.

"I'll fly out Sunday, stay the night at the airport hotel. I'll hire a car and then I'll see you early Monday morning, and I'll stay with you as long as you need me."

"What about your patients?"

"Maureen, even a shrink has personal emergencies."

Twelve ∼∞∞∾

ESMERALDA PRICHARD took over as the doyenne of the Dr. Alan Harrison household: she cooked, she cleaned, she provided all the services, she was the lady in charge. On Sunday Dr. Harrison called the school principal and arranged for Laura and Joshua to have a week off from school. The principal readily agreed. Dr. Harrison then asked that his own Diana also have that week off: she was the best friend of the Blair twins. The principal agreed again.

"Thank you," Dr. Harrison said.

"Think nuthin' of it," the principal said.

On Monday, at eight-thirty in the morning, the Harrison bell rang, and Essie Prichard answered. It was a Hiram Varney, his big van parked outside in the driveway.

"Chief Nolan," Varney said, "told me to come talk to the lady about gates in her house."

"You're early, don't you think?"

"No," Varney said. "The chief said *early* Monday mornin'. Besides, so recent a widder lady, she don't figure to sleep too good."

He was right. Maureen was not asleep.

Dr. Samuel Vaughn, in a beat-up Chevy coupe, arrived at ten o'clock. Joshua gravely introduced him to Diana Harrison and to Essie Prichard, and then Maureen introduced him to Alan Harrison, and was pleased that almost immediately they seemed to take to one another, chatting animatedly.

At noontime they were a procession rolling out of Acheron Falls: Maureen with Josh and Laura in the station wagon, Alan Harrison in his Buick with Diana, Dr. Sam in his rented Chevy coupe and Hiram Varney, the gate man, in his heavily laden van. Maureen drove slowly, and it was almost one o'clock when they arrived at the tall gaunt rectangular house standing alone against the sky.

They parked the cars in the dirt road outside the house and gathered in the kitchen, where Maureen served coffee. But the kids declared that they were hungry; Maureen looked at the clock and served lunch for everybody. Then, with more coffee, they repaired to the recreation room, all except Hiram Varney, who went about his business.

Thirteen ∽∞∝

ALAN WAS wonderful during those first awful days, but it was Dr. Samuel Vaughn who held her in balance. He brought her gently up short whenever she was tempted to slide off to self-pity. "Not you," he said, "you can't afford that luxury. Not when you're the bulwark for a Josh and a Laurie, who lost one set of parents through tragic accident, and now Steve . . ."

They found Steve's will and his life-insurance policy in a metal box in a closet in his bedroom. The will was a simple affair: whatever he owned he left to Maureen: should she predecease him, then whatever he owned he left to Laura and Joshua, share and share alike. He did not want a funeral or burial. He wished to be cremated and his ashes dispersed over the sea.

The insurance policy, with Maureen as beneficiary, was in the face value of $100,000. "It'll be twice that sum," Dr. Sam said quietly. "There's a double-indemnity clause."

She was richer as a widow than she had been as a wife.

On Wednesday the county authorities returned the body to the funeral parlor in Acheron Falls, and Dr. Sam took over with all necessary arrangements, including a helicopter that dropped the ashes over the Atlantic Ocean.

On Wednesday evening after a quiet dinner, Dr. Sam led Maureen up the stairs to Steve's study and closed the door. "A life is finished," he said, "but you must go on. There are practical matters, necessary to discuss. Time for you to come home," he said. "Time for you to leave this Godforsaken place; there's no longer any purpose; no sabbatical for Steven Blair; time for you to come back home. We'll put this old house up for sale—"

"No."

"Why not, Maureen?"

"I told you before. I can't do this to the kids. I can't keep uprooting them. They're in school here and they like it and they've made new friends here and they like them. They should stay the year in school here. It would be wrong to yank them out again just because I would like to go home."

She was not, of course, telling the whole truth. If they went home now the kids would be losing only six months, and they were bright enough to make that up in school in New York City. Nor had they made new friends here. They had made a single friend, Diana Harrison. She was lying to Dr. Sam and she knew why.

Dr. Alan Harrison.

On Friday, with best wishes from Maureen and family, Dr. Samuel Vaughn climbed into his rented Chevy and took off toward the aircraft that would fly him home.

And on Sunday Maureen said to Alan, "Your turn. You and Diana have been here now a week. It's time you went back to work; and time I settled in here alone with my children like I'm supposed to."

Harrison looked at her. She looked back at him.

"I'm not afraid," she said. "Honest to God I'm not, Alan. There's a madman loose, but I'm no more vulnerable than anyone—even you. The man is apparently a crazy, a real crazy. An insane man does not go about picking his spots, selecting the lonely faraway house where a widow now dwells alone with her two children. He picked poor old Clare Selwyn and she cetainly was not living alone. And he randomly picked a man fishing off the rocks of a breakwater jutting into the sea . . ."

Alan drew her to him and for the first time he kissed her, full on the mouth.

She sank in his arms.

"I love you."

She did not answer, except to dig herself deeper into his chest.

He drove home with Diana, thinking about himself and Maureen. The timing of his new approach was hardly ideal. What would she think?

As soon as he got home, he called her.

"I'm sorry," he said.

"Sorry? What happened?"

"Wrong moment, wrong time. I'm not making sense."

She pulled him out of it. "Yes, you are. I know what you're trying to say to me."

"God, I love you."

This time there was an answer. It came across in a whisper. "I love you too. I love you, Alan," she said, and hung up.

There was no more talk of love. Not now. She drove the children to school every day, and picked them up every day. She shopped, she cooked, she took care of her house. "I have to do what I have to do," she told him, and herself.

"You're not afraid there alone in the house?"

"When I'm alone, really alone, I have locked gates and locked doors. And when the kids are home, I have him." She pointed at blond beautiful Josh. "He's so strong."

"You're telling me?" The kid was a powerhouse. He regularly defeated Alan at tennis, handball, wrist wrestling, and Indian wrestling.

"I'd say," Maureen said, "I'm almost as protected in my home as you are in yours."

"I guess I can't disagree too much with that. I just wish you were nearer to me."

"I'm near to you, believe me."

And then on a Sunday morning in October, at seven-thirty, the doorbell rang at the Harrison house, tentative, one short ring, and Alan Harrison, a light sleeper, quickly got out of bed. Laura was staying over with Diana and he did not want the kids awakened by one of his early-morning hypochondriac patients. He went barefoot to the window, looked down.

He was looking at Mitchell Ranson.

He lifted the window, leaned out. "Be with you in a minute," he called down softly.

He lowered the window, put on a robe and slippers, went out, stopped at Diana's room and listened at the door. The girls were apparently asleep.

He started for the stairs, then turned back to a room that had once been his father's bedroom. He reached up to a high shelf in a closet and brought out a hard object wrapped in chamois. He undid the chamois and flung it away, slipped the object into a pocket of his robe. It was a Smith & Wesson automatic that had once belonged to his father. "Any state-of-Mainer worth his salt," his father would say, "has to have a gun in the house to protect his family." As a state-of-Mainer, Alan had kept his father's gun in the house and he had kept it clean and oiled and in good repair.

He ran down the stairs, opened the door and stood looking at Mitchell Ranson. The man did not look like a fugitive. Mitch was sunburned, his face freshly shaved; he was wearing a black turtleneck sweater, jeans, thick shoes, a mackinaw jacket and a sailor's watch cap. The strange eyes looked surprised.

"Hi, Mitch."

"I didn't expect *you* here."

"Whom *did* you expect?"

"Your dad."

"Dad's retired and gone south and I'm here. I took over his practice."

"You a doctor like your dad?"

"Yes."

"I remember. You always wanted to be a doctor."

131

"I'm a doctor."

"Good for you." Mitch, a burly man, crossed the threshold, kicked the door shut and embraced Alan. "I'm glad it's you. A break for me. Now I think I'll make it, now I think I'm home safe."

"Come in, Mitch." Alan led him to the living room. "Sit down, Mitch. Would you like something? Coffee? A bite to eat? Breakfast?"

"No, thank you."

"Sit down."

Mitch sat. Harrison sat near. Mitch took the knitted hat off his head and rolled it nervously in his fingers. "I don't know if you know, Alan, but they called me a loony. Put me away in Portland in a facility—that's the fancy word for lunatic asylum."

"I heard about it."

"I busted out, which was a real stupid thing to do."

"Why'd you do it?"

"Tell you the truth, I don't know. Impulse, I guess."

"Why didn't you go back?"

He grinned. The strange eyes danced. "Once I was out, I wanted a vacation. I bounced around, but I knew where I was heading. Orcus Beach. You know?"

Alan knew. Orcus Beach, eight miles south of Acheron Falls, was a wealthy community, but not in fact a Maine community. It was inhabited by foreigners. Orcus Beach, typically Maine, near the ocean but with a mountainous background of wild forest, had been settled long ago by out-of-towners, mostly New Yorkers and some Bostonians. The state of Maine was divided into counties, cities, towns, incorporated villages—and "places." Some of the places were more important to the state of Maine than some of its counties, cities, towns and villages. A "place" did not have a municipal government and it did not have a post office; the post office for Orcus Beach was Acheron Falls. But everybody in Acheron Falls knew that anybody in Orcus

Beach could buy up the whole damn town of Acheron Falls and sell it back, probably at a profit, to the state of Maine.

The dwellers of Orcus Beach, a part of a clan that moved about in quiet no-publicity places all over the world, were the basic old-money multimillionaires. The first settler in Orcus Beach, before it was known by that name or any other name, had been a relative of the fabulous Mellons. He had discovered the area—its marvelous fishing, its hunting, its privacy—and he had purchased land and built a small no-publicity mansion. Friends of the Mellons, and friends of theirs, interested in the bountiful fresh air, the beautiful scenery, the fishing, the hunting and the privacy, had purchased land and built mansions, until one Adam Rothschild Orcus, an international banker, had suggested to the others that they buy up all the surrounding real estate and thereby insure permanent privacy for themselves and their families. At that time there were twenty-two mansions, widely separated, in the place that became known as Orcus Beach, and no more mansions were built.

But they were still foreigners, itinerants, intermittent visitors. Some came and stayed for a week, some two weeks, some for a month or two, and then they were gone to their other places; but in the summer most of the Orcus Beach mansions were closed, because in the summer it was fashionable for multimillionaires to meet and mingle and live it up in such places as Paris, London, Rome, Geneva, Berlin, Copenhagen, Amsterdam, Monaco . . .

"I busted into the Fairmont place," Mitch Ranson was saying. "I did it quiet, just kind of broke a lock and slipped in. The Fairmonts, y'know? They got a history, y'know? Never missed a summer in Europe, am I right, Alan?"

"Right."

"I had my vacation," Mitch said. "They have a rack of beautiful hunting guns in that mansion and the best fishing equipment, and the rich don't bother to cut off the utilities. There's always gas and electricity and even the phones work.

133

Anyway, I fished for fish and I shot game and I cooked the stuff in a stainless-steel kitchen. And I had wine with my meals from out of the Fairmont cellar. In a restaurant you would have to pay a hundred dollars a bottle."

He stopped speaking. He twirled the navy blue watch cap in his fingers, then began to pluck at it, unraveling it. His eyelids were down, his face was without expression. He seemed almost asleep, except for the active fingers tearing at the watch cap.

"Mitch."

The eyes opened. The pupils were glazed.

Harrison said, "What do you want, Mitch?"

"I'm so glad it's you." They eyes went down again, watching the fingers tearing apart the knitted cap.

"Mitch."

"What?"

"Why, Mitch? Why are you glad?"

"You won't let them hurt me. You'll protect me. You'll take me in and I'll go with you, because I know you won't let them gun me down. That's the kind of guy your old man was. No funny stuff. That's why I came here."

"But you just told me how good you had it out there at the Fairmont mansion."

"Don't play dumb with me, Alan. You know comes October, people can come back. They got a TV there. They got TVs all over the mansion. I watch, I listen, I know what I'm up to. Comes October, I know the vacation is over . . ." He was crying.

Harrison went to the kitchen, came back with a towel, tossed it to Mitch Ranson.

Mitch wiped his face, dropped the towel to the floor. "Tell the truth, I don't like it on the outside, Alan. I'm a fruitcake, Alan, I know where I belong. I like to be protected. I need to be. They tell you when to go to sleep, when to get up, what to eat, what to drink, what you can do, movies, the TV. It's all worked out for you. Not a worry in the world."

"Then why did you break out?"

"I told you. For a lark, on an impulse. Hey, is a fruitcake supposed to be rational?" Mitch laughed, a senseless cackle, insane, and Alan was not ashamed that he had a gun in a pocket of his bathrobe.

"October," Mitch Ranson said. "Time to go back to what they call the facility"—he smiled—"and what I call the crazy house. But that's not too easy to do, Alan. When you've busted out you're a fugitive, and when you're a fugitive they shoot at you—so it's a problem. How do you get back in one piece?"

"By getting someone you trust, and having that someone take you in."

"Will you do that, Alan?"

"Is that why you went first to Clare Selwyn?"

"Who?"

"Clare Selwyn. An old-timer like my dad. Someone you could trust. Did you go to see Clare?"

"Think I did." The raveled watch cap was twirling in the fingers again. "Yeah, but that was a while ago. Yeah, an old lady, but a lady you could trust. Figured I'd talk over plans with her. About your old man. Whether she agreed with me that it should be Doc Harrison to take me in . . . like, y'know, protective custody . . . ?"

"What did she say?"

"Don't remember." The eyes were not in focus.

"Remember anything?"

"I remember she was very nice. I remember I kissed her . . ." Then Mitch was mumbling, and then he was silent.

"Mitch!"

"Yes, Alan?"

"What else do you remember about Clare."

"Clare? Nothing. I told you all I remember."

"What about the man fishing? That's more recent. A cove. A seawall of rocks, a breakwater. You must have had an argument. You hit him in the head. You cut his throat

135

with his own fishing knife?" Alan was taking a chance and knew it.

Mitch looked puzzled. "Could be, but that one I don't remember at all. No . . . I had a lot of arguments with guys out fishing, and I busted a few of them around, but hitting a man in the head and cutting the throat . . . it's possible, I mean it could be if he provoked me enough, but I really don't remember." He sighed. "Say, there's a hell of a lot I don't remember . . ." Now the tears were running again. "What are we waiting for. You know why I'm here, Alan. Please get me to Portland." He stopped crying. The planes of his face gathered to a shrewd expression. "How're we going to do it, Alan? How're you going to get me safe and sound to my facility in Portland?"

"Marcus Nolan."

"That son of a bitch."

"I'm glad you remember. You remembered my dad, you remembered Clare Selwyn. I was hoping you would remember the guy who's been chief of police since you and I were kids."

"The son of a bitch will shoot me down dead."

"No, he won't, not unless he has an excuse, like resisting arrest. I'll be bringing you in. So he won't be shooting at you. He'll ask a lot of questions for the record, but he knows he really doesn't have authority in your case. You're for the state and county people, and I'll stay with you, I promise, until those people come for you. I'm going to make the call now to Chief Nolan. Okay?"

"Whatever you say."

Alan walked slowly toward the phone and dialed Marcus Nolan at home and told him. He held the receiver close to his ear as Chief Nolan replied. Then Alan said loudly, "Yes, chief. Okay. You'll be in the station house in a few minutes waiting for us." And then he said even more loudly, "Please remember, chief, that Mitch has come in voluntarily, and that he's placed himself in my hands to take him in because

136

he trusts me and I'm going to be with him and stay with him all the way. Good-bye."

"You told him real good."

"Let's get going, Mitch."

Mitch seemed to think it normal that his driver was in pajamas, bathrobe and bedroom slippers . . .

Chief Nolan, resplendent in formal raiment, was waiting outside the station house. Alan parked at the curb and the chief approached, his Stetson hat square on his head, his revolver in his right hand, a pair of handcuffs in his left.

Mitch Ranson, wrists extended, met him halfway.

Wordlessly the chief clapped the handcuffs over Mitch's wrists and they marched, all three, into the station house. No words were exchanged, not until Mitch was behind the bars of the lockup. Then Alan told his story.

"Now, chief, I'd like to go home and get dressed. Also like to call Essie to come over to the house. I've got a couple of kids there alone. Diana and Mrs. Blair's daughter Laura. I'll wait there till Essie comes."

"No hurry."

"Then I'll get back here."

"No hurry," the chief said. "I gotta call the county and the state, and then I gotta call the funny farm in Portland. They'll all be flyin' in on the double. And then I'll be callin' Miz Blair to bring in her young fella."

"Please wait till I'm back before you make that call."

"You'll be back a long time. I ain't callin' no Miz Blair till all them officials is right here, so's her boy can make the identification in front of all of them. The kid will do it once and that will be the last for him."

"That's good of you, chief."

"Why not? That young fella's a brave one, done his duty a hunnerd percent."

Fourteen ∞

THE MAINE sky was high and blue, there were no clouds, the sun was tilted to the west. It was three o'clock and Maureen and Joshua Blair were out on the spacious front lawn, raking in the myriad October leaves, bagging them and carrying the bags to the concrete walk on the north side where, come Wednesday, the sanitation department men would take them away together with the garbage in the covered metal cans in the sunken holes.

Maureen Blair, embracing against her belly a huge, fully filled plastic bag, was near the house, almost at the north walk, when she heard the phone ring.

"The phone," she called behind her to Josh far out in front on the lawn. "Answer the phone."

"What phone?" he called back to her.

"The phone is ringing."

"I don't hear any phone ringing."

"Get in there and answer the phone, Josh. I can't, I've got my hands full."

Josh dropped his rake and sprinted to the house. Maureen tottered to the concrete walk, let the bag slide down against the wooden wall of the house and stood there with her mouth open, sucking breath, filling her lungs.

Josh came out. "You were right."

"What about?"

"The phone ringing."

"Of course. You must be getting deaf in your old age."

He laughed. "I was too far out front. And the door was closed."

"So? What's up?"

"It's for you."

"Did you take the message? Tell them I'd call back?"

"No."

She kicked the plastic bag. She rubbed dirty hands against a dirty face. "Look at me, for God's sake. Am I in condition to answer a phone? What is the matter with you today?"

"It's Chief Nolan."

"Oh." She brushed fingers against his rumpled blond hair. "I'm sorry."

He did an imitation of the local dialect . . . "Think nuthin' of it."

She put her arm through his and they went together into the house. In the kitchen she took up the dangling receiver of the wall phone. "Hello?"

"Miz Blair?"

"This is she."

The chief liked that.

"Chief Nolan?"

"This is he."

"Chief, I've spent most of this day raking leaves. I'm tired. I'm sure you didn't call to play games with me on the phone—"

"No, ma'am. What I called, it's very important, and I didn't want to mention to the boy. What I called, Miz Blair, we have apprehended the nut that killed your husband, and we need the boy, for once and for all time, to make the identification person-to-person. What I'm after is that your boy do it this once and it is the last time. What I'm after is that he don't get pestered. It's this once, the last time, and he never has to do it again. You unnerstand what I mean, Miz Blair?"

"Yes, I think—"

"I have got all the bigwigs gathered right here in our

station house. I have got our county executive. I have got the attorney general of the state of Maine. I have got the director of the Portland hospital for the criminal insane. And the director has brought with him Dr. Eugene Lubeck who was Ranson's personal shrink up there at the funny farm. Mitchell Ranson, ma'am. That is the kook, the guy that done the murder—"

"May I call Dr. Harrison? I would like him to be present, if you don't mind."

"He is present, ma'am. He is right here. Would you like to talk with him?"

And then Alan was on the phone and telling her what had happened.

"All right, we'll see you soon," she said, and hung up and went to Josh. "Josh . . . they've caught the man that killed dad."

"Oh, boy . . . that's *good*."

"They want you to make a personal identification."

"Yes. Sure."

She pulled him against her, kissed his forehead. "You're one brave young man."

"What's so brave to identify your father's murderer? When do they want us?"

"Right away."

They went upstairs to shower and dress.

And driving into town she told him what Alan had told her.

Josh listened with half-closed eyes, his head turned toward his window, a hint of a smile on his lips.

In the crowded room, all eyes were on the boy. He stood tall, white blond hair almost glowing, clear blue eyes. He looked back at all the people looking at him.

"This young man is Joshua Blair," Chief Nolan said. "What you're gonna do for us today, son, is what you have done before—ID. But this time it's gonna be a face-to-face. Okay?"

140

"Yes, sir."

"Officer Putnam," Nolan called.

Officer Putnam stepped forward and actually saluted.

"Bring the prisoner, please."

Officer Putnam performed a brisk about-face and marched off. Five minutes later he came back with Mitchell Ranson, whose wrists were now handcuffed behind his back. Officer Putnam arranged Mitch alongside his poster-size photo on the wall.

Mitch Ranson, leaning against his poster, looked out at his audience, his glazed eyes making no contact until he saw Dr. Eugene Lubeck.

"Hey, doc. Hey, Lubeck. Hey, how are you?"

Lubeck, small and round, trudged forward and stood near Ranson. "This won't take long, Mitchell. Necessary formalities, but we've been promised that they'll be done quickly. You'll soon be back where you belong, safe and sound."

"Hey, thank you, doc."

"Mr. Attorney General," Chief Nolan said, "this young man, Joshua Blair, has heretofore identified by photo that Mitchell Ranson is the perpetrator who committed the homicide of Mr. Steven Blair. Officer Putnam will now read Joshua's sworn statement, which Joshua will verify in your presence."

Officer Putnam read the sworn statement.

"You have identified the photograph as the man who killed your father?" Nolan said.

"I have."

"Do you see that man now? Here in person?"

"I do."

"Point to him."

Josh pointed to Mitchell Ranson.

"Now there is the additional matter of the homicide of the woman Clare Selwyn—"

"No, that's enough." Dr. Eugene Lubeck moved in front of Ranson. "We have Dr. Harrison's affidavit about that matter. This man, my patient Mitchell Ranson, can neither affirm nor deny; he is not competent, as the attorney general knows, to affirm or deny. He has already been sentenced to spend the rest of his life with us at Portland Hospital. So I suggest he be released to the director and myself and we take him home."

Chief Nolan looked at the attorney general, who nodded and said what a hell of a job he had done.

And then they were gone; their cars roared off, trailed by the sound of wailing sirens.

In Chief Nolan's office now, the chief said to Josh, "Let me tellya, Joshua, you are the hero of this whole damn business. Never mind the attorney general throws me the compliment. That's politics. I played ball with him, so he did it for me with the media present."

"Dr. Harrison is the hero," Josh said.

Nolan laughed. "He brung him in, but what's the hero? The guy came to him—they was kids together—and the guy says to deliver him without no bloodshed and that's what the doc does. But you, a young boy witness to the killin' of your father. And you hold your head together to see who done it and remembered the poster you saw here and you told your mama right off who the guy was."

"Josh has my vote too," Harrison said.

"Gentlemen, enough," Maureen said. "You're embarrassing him."

Josh good-humoredly denied it. "Don't stop them, mom. I'm loving it."

Everybody laughed, then Nolan said, "Okay, we got this crazy out of our hair, but don't you let your guard down, Miz Blair. Not out there in that old house, you alone with two kids. You keep them gates up over the windows and be sure you lock up tight when you go to sleep."

"Enough for this Sunday," Harrison said. "If you want any of us later on"—Harrison's gesture was a circular sweep—"we'll all be home in my house."

142

It had been a good idea. Driving home with the children on Monday after school, Maureen reflected on the wisdom of Alan's suggestion that they all stay together on Sunday and sleep over. She knew what Alan was after, a kind of therapy, and it had worked pretty well. They had played games, or at least played at them, and then the kids had gone to bed early. After seeing the kids off to school, she had had a breakfast-lunch and driven to Jackson City for some shopping. More therapy.

Driving home, she thought again about the need to give Laurie her special attention. She had noticed yesterday and then again this morning that Laurie, of the three Blairs, seemed most affected, and she thought she knew why. She and Josh had been right there in the midst of all the activity, terrible as it was, but Laurie had remained in the Harrison home. She had been out of it all, her imagination was free to run riot. Not good for the nerves.

But it was more than just yesterday. Of the three surviving Blairs it had been Laurie who had been most disturbed by Steven's death, had retreated into herself, had been subject to sudden weeping, displays of nerves. Now, a month later, Maureen thought she could understand. Laurie was the most delicate, the most sensitive of all of them. Josh was the strongest, proud of his maleness, so brave, always determined to overcome. And Maureen could reach outside of the family . . . to Alan Harrison . . .

Dr. Sam had cautioned Maureen, and after he had gone she had tried to give Laurie special attention and consideration. Over the month Laurie had seemed to improve, but yesterday was a setback. No one noticed except Maureen, and so her shopping this morning in Jackson City had been for Laurie exclusively. Steve used to say, "When in doubt about a method, start with the stomach." A variation on the way to a man's heart . . . In Jackson City this morning, Maureen had sought out and found several of Laurie's fa-

143

vorite foods: sturgeon, smoked salmon, goose-liver pâté for tidbits, a leg of veal for roasting. A real gourmet, her Laurie. A very special girl with already highly developed sensibilities.

The kids went upstairs to do homework and Maureen went to the kitchen to do cooking. "Not really homework," Josh said. "A chemistry experiment."

"Don't smell up the house," Maureen cautioned.

"Don't worry, not this time," Josh said.

"Okay, out of my kitchen, please, both of you."

But then, after she had put in her roast for cooking, Maureen went up to Laura's room. In bra and panties, Laura was stretched out on the bed, leaning on her elbows, her chin in her hands, a book on a pillow.

"Need any help?" Maureen asked.

"It's not allowed." Laura closed the book and came off the bed. "Not in reading. Parents can help with math or science or stuff like that, but not reading. At least not this reading because the homework is to interpret it, to tell what we think, what it does to us. It's a poem. Walt Whitman."

"Well, Walt Whitman, no less."

" 'When Lilacs Last In the Dooryard Bloom'd.' Isn't that beautiful, mother? The sound of that?"

Maureen's heart clenched. Always, since childhood, Laurie adored beautiful things, even beautiful sounds. Laurie came to her mother and kissed her. "It's about Abraham Lincoln's assassination. It's Whitman's poem in memory of President Lincoln. So far we're assigned only the first three stanzas to read and write a report about our interpretation."

She loved this child-woman, so perfectly formed, and she felt guilt in the awareness that she loved this one, her daughter, more than the other, her son, and immediately she rationalized . . . Josh was so strong, not so in need of love. This one was fragile, vulnerable, so terribly in need.

"Listen," Maureen said, clearing her throat, coughing to

144

cover embarrassment, "if I can't help, then what the heck am I doing here?"

"That's a good question, mother."

Of course she loved Josh too, she loved them both with all her heart . . . Dear God, I'm ashamed of myself. "Listen," she said, "you go back to your reading and interpreting and I'll go back to my cooking." She took her daughter in her arms. "You all right?"

"Yes, mother."

"I was a little worried about you."

"Please don't worry."

"All that terrible business yesterday."

"I was a little shook, but I'm better, really. I think Mr. Walt Whitman helped a lot."

It was a fine dinner. Laura said, "I know you did this one especially for me. It had *everything* I love."

"Me too," Josh said.

"You." Laura said. "You love everything."

"I did it for both of you," Maureen said quickly.

"Mother's a diplomat," Laura said.

Maureen cut it off by shooing them out to the TV. Alone in the kitchen, she heard herself humming. The day had turned out well, better than she had dared hope. Walt Whitman had worked for Laurie and the dinner had put a cap on it. Humming, Maureen cleared the table and cleaned the plates for the dishwasher.

The telephone rang. It was probably Alan. She wiped her hands and went to the phone. "Hello?"

A dial tone.

But the ringing continued.

Her knees turned to jelly.

She ran, stumbling, out of the kitchen and up toward the attic. She was almost there when the ringing stopped.

She opened the attic door.

There was no sound.

145

Fifteen ∾∾∾

Folie à deux.

A psychiatric term, she had heard it long ago, and had even discussed it with Steve and Dr. Sam. *Folie à deux*, the madness of two, a double-header, a psychotic syndrome in which two persons intimately associated—like a husband and wife—come to share the same delusions. Well, she would have none of it. A toy phone could *not* ring by itself. She told it to herself again and again. It can only happen in the mind, an aural hallucination, *and she would have none of it.*

It happened once more in that month of October. They were in her bedroom watching television, she and the children, when the phone rang, and she was immediately alert, because there was no reaction from the kids. Nothing, no movement, not a flicker. Casually she got up and went to the phone, put the receiver to her ear. There was no one on the other end. But the ringing continued.

"What's up?" Laura said.

"I thought I heard the phone." Maureen cradled the receiver.

Josh said, "It was a phone on the TV."

"I often make that mistake too," Laura said.

"Sure," Maureen said.

But a phone was still ringing, loudly, insistently. Maureen tried to shake it off. *Folie à deux.* No, not me. I refuse . . . She remembered a conversation with Steve after breakfast. They were alone, a Saturday, the kids at the Harrison

146

house. They were talking over coffee, Steve about the supernatural, she—informed by Dr. Sam—thinking about aural hallucination. On one point there had been agreement. Only *he* could hear the ringing that called him to the little red phone. Now—*folie à deux*—only *she* could hear the ringing.

She resumed her seat and steadfastly watched the show on the television. She sat crunched forward, hearing the ringing, fighting it—and then at last it stopped.

She told herself it was over for good. She had fought it off, she had won. No more crazy ringing from a little toy phone, no more remnant from Steve's delusion.

And there was no more ringing in the month of October, and nothing as the days went by in November . . .

Weekends they stayed with Alan. He'd insisted. "At least now at the beginning," he had said to Maureen, "until you and the kids begin to get used to living alone out there . . ."

They loved it. Laurie enjoyed being with Diana. Josh was happy exploring the town and its environs, and his games—especially the athletic ones—with Alan. And Maureen loved it because she was in love with Alan Harrison.

Their sleeping quarters, by habit pattern, became arranged. It was a three-bedroom house. Laurie slept with Diana in Diana's bedroom, Harrison in the master bedroom and Maureen in the guest bedroom. Josh slept downstairs on a divan in the living room.

Alan and Maureen came close but somehow managed to stay out of each other's bed. They'd made a pact based on an old tradition: a year must pass before the widow can take to herself a new husband. Two modern people rooted in principles of the past.

But they were not solemn. Alan made her laugh, sparked her spirits, kept her up. Each weekend they were like a family with the children, and that helped.

But it wasn't easy. Not by a long shot. They were, after all, only human.

On a Saturday night in November the phone rang in Dr. Alan Harrison's bedroom, waking him. It was one o'clock. "What?" he said into the mouthpiece.

"Dan Corely here." Corely was Chief Nolan's second deputy. His first deputy was Oscar Putnam.

"Yes, Dan, what is it?"

"Sorry to wake you, doc—"

"What is it?"

"Looks like we got a homicide."

"Who?"

"Chief Nolan."

"My God . . . where? . . . how? . . ."

"Station house. Please get down here right away. You're my first call, doc, and I'm not callin' no one else till you get here, not even his missus."

"I'm on my way."

Going out he was careful not to wake Josh on the divan in the living room.

The Acheron Falls police department comprised fifteen men—fourteen officers and the chief of police. There was no rank—no sergeants, no lieutenants—but there were two deputy chiefs.

From 8:00 A.M. to 4:00 P.M. four men were out on patrol and two men were in the station house. At 4:00 P.M. the new shift came on: four for patrol and two for the station house. At midnight, the new shift, the 12:00 A.M. to 8:00 A.M. was smaller: two men out on patrol and one man in the station house. As Ozzie Putnam would say, "After midnight in Acheron Falls nuthin' stirs except the owls." The men, including Marcus Nolan, rotated the shifts, changing each week.

This week the in-house night man at the station was Chief Nolan.

Dan Corely was waiting outside as Alan Harrison parked the car. They went quickly to the station house, where in the outer room a young cop, Dick Wilbur, stood leaning against a wall, eyes blank. "You stay right where you are," Corely said. "Just breathe deep, try to pull yourself together. This way, doc."

The late Chief Marcus Nolan was seated in the swivel chair behind his desk. For once he was not wearing his Stetson hat; it was lying askew on the floor near him. The chief's face was tilted upward; his sightless eyes were fixed on the ceiling; his throat was a red hole, blood still coming from it. His face, drained of blood, was alabaster white. His uniform was like a butcher's apron.

Corely said, "We was out on patrol, Dick and me. We come in at midnight, and this was our first turn. You know how we work the nighttime, doc . . ." Two men in a patrol car, one man in the station house. The two men patrol for an hour; if necessary they radio in to the station house, and the man in the station house calls out to get them help if necessary. This night that man was the chief. Every hour on the hour the men come in from patrol to the station house for coffee or to use the bathroom. Later in the night they come in for the quick meal they brownbagged in, then out again on the hour-to-hour patrol until the change up with their relief squad at 8:00 A.M.

"We come in at midnight, which is also the chief's tour of duty this week in the station house. We clown around a little with the chief, then me and Dick go out in the prowl car. We come back like one o'clock to make our report, which is nuthin', and maybe to grab a little java . . . and what you see right here, this is what we found . . . I looked around a little and then first off called you."

"What do you make of it?" Harrison said.

"Only one thing I can tell you. The guy that did this was no stranger to the chief. Chief Nolan weren't born yesterday, he was a pretty smart piece of goods. Look at the way he's sittin' there in his chair, nice and comfy. And look there." Corely pointed to the chief's gun belt. "His gun is in there in the holster, and the holster is buttoned down. Somebody come in here, but it was somebody the chief trusted, and that's the somebody who cut his throat wide open."

"With what?"

"A knife, what else?"

"Any sign of one?"

"No, sir, and there ain't gonna be. We got a lot of ocean around here. Anybody shrewd enough to put this over on the chief is shrewd enough to drown his knife where nobody can ever find it again. It had to be somebody the chief knew and trusted."

"Tell me more, Dan." Alan was impressed.

Corely pointed to the Stetson on the floor. "The chief was wearin' his hat, that you and me can both swear, right, doc? But he ain't wearin' it now, is he? He didn't take it off and just throw it to the floor, did he? So I say this here happened . . . Whoever is here, he is talkin' to the chief very nice and smooth. He talks, and walks, and talks, and keeps walkin' around. And then, talkin', he is behind the chief—and then his left hand does a stranglehold on the chief and the right hand, with the knife, comes around and slits the throat. Just look at what you see there, doc, and you will understand what I mean. The stranglehold from behind knocked off the Stetson, and there it is on the floor. The stranglehold twisted the head up, and there he is, the chief, still starin' at the ceiling. You get the picture, doc?"

"Too well. But can you add to that picture?"

"Like how?"

"Who would want to kill him? Who that the chief knew and trusted, would let move around behind him . . . who like that would want to kill him?"

"No idea."

It was five in the morning when he got home and knocked on the door of Maureen's bedroom, knocked lightly, but kept knocking until she answered.

"What's the matter?"

150

"I have to talk to you."

Fright made her voice thin. "The children . . . ?"

"No."

"What?"

"I can't tell you through the door."

"A minute," she said.

When she opened she looked so young, no makeup, her hair piled on her head, her body shapeless inside one of his bathrobes.

"May I come in?" he said. "I can't take you downstairs to the living room. Josh is sleeping there."

She looked even younger, the surprise on her face, at seeing him fully dressed at five in the morning.

"What's the matter?"

He pushed through, closed the door behind him. And he told her about Dan Corely's call, and about Marcus Nolan.

"I debated whether to wake you and decided yes because of the children. We have to talk now because we're going to have to tell them early. Tomorrow's Sunday, the news will be all over town and we can't let them learn about it that way."

"No. We'll do it at breakfast." She put a hand to his face. "You look so tired."

"I've had a busy night."

Back in bed, she thought about Marcus Nolan. She remembered how the big man in the Stetson hat had protected Josh, how kind he had been to the boy, shielding him, and how at the end he had praised him and declared him to be the hero.

But what was happening here?

She got out of bed and sat hunched by the window, watching as the sunrise put its polish on the windowpanes of the neighborhood. *What was happening here in Acheron Falls?* In all the years—going back to the time of Jack and Nina Mercer—this tiny little town had been a quiet, lovely,

151

sleepy little place. What had happened? What was happening here in these past few months? An eighty-year-old woman had been raped and murdered. Steven had been smashed in the head and cut to death. A homicidal lunatic had roamed the town, had turned himself in and been taken away. But now another man was dead. They had found Chief Nolan at his desk, his throat slashed too, like Steve's . . . What in God's name was happening? Why had a sleepy little town suddenly turned into a hell?

Maybe she should do as Dr. Sam had said. Scoop up the kids, turn tail on this suddenly crazy place and rush back to the impersonal cocoon of New York City. She sat there, hands tightly clasped, realizing she was being silently hysterical . . . She loved Alan Harrison and wanted him to be her husband. She loved his child Diana. She could not turn her back on them and run. She sighed, slapped at her knees, stood up from the window and went back to bed.

Sleep did not come.

Sixteen ∿∞∿

ON A MONDAY morning in the middle of November, the town council, township of Acheron Falls, sat in City Hall to appoint a new chief of police. Presiding was the council's president, Dr. Ronald Harvey, who had invited Dr. Alan Harrison to sit in as an observer.

It had been anticipated that the proceedings would be brief. The late Chief Nolan had set up an orderly line of succession in the event of his departure from office: first choice was First Deputy Oscar Putnam, second was Second Deputy Daniel Corely. The vote went as expected, unanimous for Oscar Putnam, until Dr. Harvey abruptly invoked "moral impropriety" against Putnam, explaining that he was sad to say that a patient of his, to be nameless, had told him that the deputy, to her knowledge, had been carrying on an affair with a cocktail waitress in Jackson City, where the patient also made her residence but still came to see Dr. Harvey. Putnam lived in Acheron Falls with his wife, but was carrying on in Jackson City with the other woman, with whom he frequently stayed.

An investigative committee was named, headed by one Nicholas Hubball, proprietor of Nick Hubball's Associated Supermarket in Acheron Falls, and on Wednesday this worthy confirmed the worst against Deputy Putnam. Additionally, it was even suggested by the chief prosecutor of the county's district attorney's office, G. Arthur Thayer, that Putnam had motive and opportunity to murder his late boss—money in the new post that would double his present salary and which he desperately needed to maintain in effect two households, and opportunity through his position of being trusted by his late chief and being known to have been in town on the night of the murder. Unfortunately, Thayer also had been given sworn affadavits by not only Putnam but also by his wife that he had been with her *all* night on the fateful night and indeed the couple had spent their time in "conjugal intercourse."

So with this perfect alibi nothing could be done against Putnam, except to declare him unfit for the office and to appoint in his place Daniel Corely as chief of police of Acheron Falls. As it turned out, Oscar Putnam seemed far from a cad. He was, as he demonstrated to Dr. Alan Harrison, genuinely in love with Edith Laurel, who actually was anything but the trollop she had been represented to be, but a little lady out of Fort Lauderdale, Florida, who, though she had been around some, had fallen as completely for Putnam as he had for her. As Putnam told Harrison when he and Miss Laurel came to the doctor's office, he was sorry for the scandal and embarrassment to his wife, but there it was and to prove his good faith he handed the doctor his resignation from the police force, to be passed on to the new chief, and also handed over an envelope containing eight thousand dollars for his wife, retaining only one thousand for himself. He also left his wife the house and car free and clear. And then he and Miss Laurel hit the road south for Fort Lauderdale—a forty-nine-year-old ex-deputy, for whom life's lightning had struck one more time, and his twenty-eight-year-old lady who for no darn good reason that he could figure was as crazy about him as he was about her.

When Alan Harrison called Doctor Harvey about the matter of Oscar Putnam, Harvey quickly accepted the situation, having especially on his mind his boat which was being delivered that afternoon to the town marina. He suggested that Alan come see it, and Alan accepted promptly,

154

saying he'd also like to bring along Mrs. Blair and the kids whom they would pick up after school.

When Alan met Maureen at their bench, and picked up the kids, he filled her in on the events with Putnam, and she asked him if he believed Putnam and his wife. Did he think that maybe Mrs. Putnam had lied to protect him? Alan said he couldn't be absolutely sure, but he was pretty well convinced by the way Putnam had acted, including his decency toward his ex-wife. The man simply did not seem a possible, or reasonable, suspect any longer.

The exchange between Alan and Maureen went on briefly in the car on the way to the marina, and, of course, the kids were in the backseat, horsing around and looking forward to the adventure. If they liked, they could hear what the adults were saying, and one in particular, Josh, seemed especially interested when Alan said he did not believe Putnam was a credible suspect for the murder of the late police chief. In fact, Josh looked downright sober, in contrast to his usual ebullience when around Alan, who of course he felt so close to ever since the terrible death of his late stepfather, Steven Blair. It was clear to all, and Maureen was profoundly grateful for it, that in Alan, Josh had found himself a new father.

Driving back home from the marina, Maureen recalled Josh's strangely quiet behavior, and then realized it must have been a reaction to the death of Chief Nolan, who had, after all, been so nice to him, praising him as a hero in the whole business with Steve's murder and his courageous identification of the crazy man. She considered asking Josh about it, then decided it was better to leave it alone. The boy had been through enough.

Feeling she had much to be thankful for, she made the turn and drove up the hill along the dirt road toward the gaunt house silhouetted against the late afternoon sky.

Thanksgiving was a full week away, but Maureen was already making preparations. It would be a real event, a *family* event, with Alan, Diana, Esmeralda Prichard, Laurie, Josh and herself all together.

After dinner this evening Maureen continued to work in the kitchen, then cleaned up. It was late. The kids had actually turned off the TV on their own and gone to bed. Maureen went up to her room, showered, slipped into a fresh nightgown and took a book to bed. She was wide awake, and would read until she got sleepy. For some reason, though, she could not concentrate on the book. She felt strangely apprehensive. She closed the book. All right, she told herself, settle down. Every window in the house is protected by an accordian gate. The front and back doors are locked and latched.

She opened the book again and began to read—

The phone rang.

She pretended to herself it was nothing special. The phone was on the bed table beside her. She reached over, took up the receiver. Dial tone. But somewhere a phone was ringing. Loudly, insistently—and of course she knew where.

She had thought it was over.

Back in October she had fought it off, had refused to give in to it. She had prayed to God and the sound of the ringing had ceased, and she had truly believed that with God's help she had defeated it—whatever *it* was.

But here it was again. It was ringing.

She decided she had been wrong not to meet it head on.

She flung away the book, got out of bed and ran up the attic stairs. She thrust open the door, snapped on the light. The ringing was louder, more insistent. She went over to the little red phone, took it from its shelf, put the receiver to her ear. "Hello?" she said into the ridiculous little mouthpiece, feeling like a crazy person.

"Maury?"

She began to shake.

"Maury?" Steven's voice . . . it was *like* Steven's voice . . . strange, somehow hollow, somehow metallic, but it *was* Steven's voice . . . "Maury? Hello? Maury?"

The little red phone slipped from her hands to the attic floor.

She followed it in a dead faint.

Seventeen ∽∞∽

SHE LAY in bed now in absolute darkness, her eyes wide open, staring at nothing . . .

In the attic, returning to consciousness, she had rolled over on the floor, grabbed up the little phone, put the receiver to her ear. "Hello?" she had said. "*Hello?*" Of course, nothing. It was dead. Inanimate. It was a little red phone, a child's toy.

Struggling to her feet, tearing her nightgown in the process, she had restored the little red phone to its place on the shelf, then had somehow made it to the attic door, clicked off the light and gotten downstairs to her bedroom . . .

She lay rigid on her back in the darkness, still in her torn nightgown. All right, damn it, think . . . face it, no more retreat. She remembered how Steve had heard a phone ringing that no one else had heard, and he'd found that the ringing came from the little toy phone in the attic. He'd answered the ring of the toy telephone and said he had recognized Jack Mercer's voice on the other end, but the voice was so faint he couldn't make out what it was that Jack was trying to say . . . "He's trying to say *something* to me," Steve had said, "but it won't come through, he's been dead too long . . ."

And then Steve had come across that book about the telephone as a medium for communication between the living and the dead, with all sorts of so-called scientific documentation, and she had argued with him. A toy? *A toy telephone?* The dead communicating with the living by means of a *toy* telephone? And his reply . . . "If the dead can talk, and they can talk to you through the Bell telephone, why can't they talk to you through a toy telephone?" All right, if . . . But she remembered most of all what had been maybe his most important argument . . . that Jack Mercer had been dead for too long, which explained why his voice had been too faint to get through. Jack had wanted to tell him something but couldn't get through. And Steve had died, horribly—my God, was there a connection? And now, the call to her from Steve . . . was *he* trying to tell her something . . . ?

Stop it, she ordered herself. But she could not dismiss the thought so easily. She could not dismiss it at all.

She lay rigid, trying to will herself to sleep. And not managing that either.

This weekend she would not stay with the kids at the Harrison house. This day, Friday, she would shop and go home to continue her preparations for Thanksgiving on Thursday and for the weekend, when all the guests would be staying over. Anyway, that was what she told Alan.

Alan, of course, protested her not coming this weekend, but she convinced him that she really needed the time at home for the Thanksgiving preparations.

Which was a lie.

She wanted to be home alone for the telephone calls—if they came.

She drove home with a carload of comestibles—some fresh, some frozen, some canned—but her prize was a big fat enormous turkey that Dora Hubball had selected and put away especially for her. She laid away the big turkey in the freezer. There was nothing really she had to do, no preparations for the Thanksgiving dinner, it was far too early for any of that. But there was work to be done in the house. She and Laurie did do cleaning, but it was a big house and the cleaning and dusting were never fully managed.

In her bedroom she undressed to bra and panties and looked at herself in a mirror. Not bad. Despite all that had happened since coming to Acheron Falls, she looked pretty good; there were a few new little lines around her eyes but not deep. She was only thirty-two.

She took out the vacuum cleaner, prepared a pail of soapy water and a pail of clean water and took out the squeeze-type sponge mop. And she decided she would start with the one room she dreaded—the attic.

She stood akimbo in the middle of the room and looked about. Sunshine streamed through the ventilation vents; there had been no need to click on the overhead lights. Long ago the Mercers had transformed it to a bright and lovely children's room. The vinyl floor was shiny pink, and the tall walls were papered with gay designs of angels flying and cherubs kissing and leprechauns grinning. All along those walls there were the shelves that contained memorabilia: Laurie's dolls, Josh's trains, piggy banks, children's books and what had once been Josh's favorite toy, the little red phone. So solid, so sturdily built, a perfect replica of a real telephone, except for the metal crank extending from its right side.

She stood in the middle of the room and looked across to the little red phone nestled in place on its shelf. She stepped away from the vacuum cleaner, the sponge mop, the dust rags, the pails of water, and walked purposefully to the toy phone. She took it from the shelf and carried it to one of the small mahogany children's tables.

She set the little red phone down in the middle of the top of one of the tables. She sat spread-legged in a little mahogany chair and stared at the toy telephone. She touched it, poking at it with an index finger.

She shivered, took up the toy, examined it. It was thick wrought, really quite substantial. She turned it over and over, peering, poking. She rotated the crank, which gave

160

off a good ring, but it was not the kind of ring that could penetrate throughout the house.

She got up from the little mahogany chair, replaced the little red phone and went to work cleaning the room. Therapy? She cleaned Josh's room. Therapy. She cleaned Laurie's room and was exhausted. She showered, went to bed and napped.

A ringing phone woke her, but somehow she knew it was not the little red phone. It was dark. She switched on the reading light, grappled with the phone on the bed table, finally got the receiver to her ear. It was Alan, who talked to her lovingly and then put on Laurie, who then put on Josh, who then put on Diana, who then put on Alan . . .

She was hungry, dead tired. She put on wool pajamas and furry house slippers and went about the house putting on lights. All alone in the big house she felt . . . fidgety. She examined windows, all the window gates were secure. And examined the front door and the back door—all locked, deadlocked. She ate in the kitchen, but sparingly; she was too damn tired. She had chewed off more than she could bite, which made her smile. She cleaned up in the kitchen and went upstairs to the study. Read a goddamn book.

Upstairs she selected Joseph Conrad's *Heart of Darkness*. She removed the furry house slippers, tucked a pillow under her head on Steve's couch, opened to the first page. Five minutes later the book fell off her chest and she was fast asleep . . .

The ringing of the phone woke her.

She ran.

She opened the attic door, snapped on the light, ran to the little red phone, took it from the shelf, put the receiver to her ear.

"Maury?"

She refused to faint.

She slid into one of the little mahogany chairs, put the phone on the little table, kept the receiver at her ear. Was she crazy? "Hello?"

"Maury?"

She must be crazy. She was sitting in a child's chair at a child's table talking through a child's toy telephone to a dead man.

"There's so much I have to tell you . . ." Steve's voice. But muffled, as though he were talking through a filter. "I won't be able to tell it all at one time. Rules. Sometimes I'll have a few minutes, sometimes only a minute, sometimes I'll only be able to say your name before we'll be disconnected. But once I tell you all you have to know, then it will be finished and you will never hear from me again."

"Tell me *what*?"

"What Jack Mercer was trying to tell me. It's my obligation now. I must tell you what Jack was trying to tell me—"

"What are you *talking* about?" (And what was *she* talking to?)

"I'm talking about Joshua Mercer Blair—"

"*You're crazy.*" She was crazy . . . listen to yourself, you crazy woman . . . yelling into a dead toy telephone, accusing a *dead* man of being crazy. Except she did not believe she was crazy. Further proof of it?

Shrewdly, she said, "Hello, Steve," into the toy telephone. No answer. Of course. She was sitting in a child's chair by a child's table, talking into a child's telephone.

Eighteen ∿∞∿

SHE WAS able to sleep this Friday night because she had figured something out.

Guilt.

In her heart, admit it, she had favored Laurie over Josh, perhaps because she felt the girl was so much more in need of loving care; perhaps because the boy twin seemed so much stronger, so much more self-sufficient. Favoritism between two equally bereft children. Of course she had to punish herself. With delusions of her late husband's sickness. So she too had heard the ringing of the toy telephone, answered the ring, heard a voice. A punishment. Through the imagined voice of the ghost. What could be more horrible than her own demonic indictment of her beautiful Josh . . .

Peace. Reason gave off comprehension, followed by blessed sleep.

A sunny, cloudless November Saturday. She had a full breakfast—juice, bacon and eggs, toast and coffee—and then leaving everything on the table she went out for a long walk.

Returning, unlocking the door, she thought she heard a phone ring. When she got in, locking the door behind her, there was no ringing.

She washed the dishes, cleaned up the kitchen.

The phone rang.

It was Laurie.

"Hi, mom."

"Hi, baby."

"I called you before. Where were you?"

"Out walking. I trust that's permissible."

"Mother, don't get grumpy, please. I was just asking."

"Okay. Anything special?"

"About what?"

"Honey, *you* called *me*."

"Didn't call about anything special. Just called my mother to ask how's my mother."

"I'm just fine and dandy. And how's my daughter?"

"Super."

"Josh?"

"Super, and so's Diana and Essie and Dr. Harrison. All send their love. Dr. Harrison told me to tell you he'll be calling you later when he's free. Do you miss us, mother?"

"I do."

"So do we."

"I love you, baby."

"I love you, mom."

Of course she was sane. Was not this a sane exchange? But if she was . . .

She went about cleaning the house again, room after room until she was exhausted, then showered, put on pajamas, went to Steve's study, stretched out on his couch and read again at *Heart of Darkness*.

At four o'clock the phone rang. It was Alan. He missed her, loved her. Likewise for her. She felt jumpy as hell.

In the evening she ate a steak. No frills. Just steak.

No phone rang.

She did cleaning. At ten to nine she went to the rec room and turned on the TV. She watched a boring one-hour show, an interesting one-hour show, at eleven she was tuned to a news program—

She heard the ringing.

She ran up to the attic, went to the ringing toy phone. She took it from the shelf, put the receiver to her ear.

"Maury?"

She began to tremble, but fought off fainting. She slid down into the child's chair by the child's table.

"Maury?"

She tried to make saliva so she could speak. "Yes. I'm here."

"I must talk fast, only a limited time to tell it so forgive my abruptness. You must not interrupt. You are not imagining. It's me, Steve. You must listen carefully, do you understand?"

"Yes, no, I mean—"

"Listen to me. Opportunities like this are rare. I will not use easy words to define what you have a unique opportunity to destroy. To do so would make this seem unserious—like you first reacted to the notion of communications like this one. But, just as when Jack Mercer kept trying to communicate with me, the conditions existed . . . *you* have the opportunity to do an important service. You have become special—"

"Conditions? Important service . . . ?"

"Conditions, Maury. Listen. No matter how disbelieving you may be, for *God's* sake *listen* . . . This . . . force to be destroyed must be in the period of puberty. That is when we can communicate for its destruction. But communication can only be made where it was born. The means of communication must be an object—a doll, mechanical toy, whatever it favored as a child and grew attached to while growing up. We can't get through unless the other side is a person we love and trust—a dear friend, close relative, husband or wife. And that person must be living there at the place where the child was born. All four conditions being met is extremely rare, which is why when the confluence happens it *must* be taken advantage of. Do you understand what I'm saying?"

"I don't know, I think—"

"Most babies are born in a hospital. But Josh was born right there in the house where you are. When Jack Mercer passed over he learned what was happening but had to wait until the puberty period, and then he tried but wasn't able to get his message through to me—"

"Just a minute—"

"I don't have much more time now—"

"Why are you singling out Josh? Oh God . . . I mean why am *I* creating all this in my imagination—?"

"*Not* your imagination. You are *not* creating—"

"What about the other? His twin? What about Laurie? Do we have another force or whatever the hell it is in Laurie? A female of the species? They're supposed to be the deadlier species, you know—"

"No. Stop it, Maury. Don't try to be light about this, and don't be confused. Now listen to me. I will continue to call. Before I have finished I will, piece-by-piece, give you a great deal of information. But none of it concerns Laura. It is only about Josh—"

She heard her voice, nasal, sardonic. "Only Josh? Really? Was he too much for you? A little boy already more of a man than you were?"

"Maury, you must help me. He's already working on you, trying to confuse you, turn you against me. Turn you against Laura. I beg you, Maury, it has nothing to do with Laura even though she's a twin. She is a normal human being. Josh is not . . ."

And the phone went dead.

In the child's chair, she sat and looked at it.

"Hello?" she said into the little red phone.

Nothing. Once more a toy telephone. She shook it, banged it against the table, turned the crank handle and shouted into the silly little mouthpiece. No answer. Of course not.

Poor Maureen. Linked to her dead husband by Dr. Sam's *folie à deux*. Fancy talk for plain crazy. Right, Maureen? She shook her head, sighed and pushed herself up from squatting in a child's chair by a child's table in the long rectangular attic.

166

Nineteen ∽∞∾

THE PHONE did not ring on Sunday. God's day? Was it giving her a day of rest? Or did Steve know there on the other side that company was coming?

Get it out of your mind for now at least. She had work to do. Dinner for six. A fish dinner. Alan had taken Josh fishing on Harvey's new boat, and Essie had taken Diana and Laura skiing on Mt. Snow. They'd all be here.

The phone rang. The real phone.

It was afternoon.

"How are you?" Alan said. "We have fish, darling."

"Well, I didn't think you'd have moose. So when are you coming?"

"An hour?"

"Make that an hour and a half?"

It gave her time to bathe, and wash and dry her hair. She did her makeup carefully. She selected a good dress, a New York creation that had been made to order for her by a young Greenwich Village dressmaker, designed to be worn without a bra. Why not? Her morale could use it.

They piled out of Dr. Harrison's Buick, the girls and Essie. Josh and Alan were busy with the trunk of the car, taking out a flat metal bin of fish on ice and carrying it into Maureen's kitchen.

"Quite a day, quite a day," Harrison said. "What we have here is somewhat of a variety, and a lot of it you'll have to freeze. We have two mackerel, each eighteen inches

167

long; we have four fat blue fish; but what we have most of all, is Josh's catch, which was a forty-pound cod, now nicely sliced into thick steaks."

"Forty pounds." Maureen meant to sound more excited. She quickly smiled at Josh and ruffled his hair.

It was a fine dinner.

Soon afterward Essie went up for a nap and did not come back, and the girls were tired too, nodding off in the recreation room as they watched television. But Josh insisted on showing some experiments to Alan, and Maureen went along.

Josh heated a blue liquid until it became colorless, then after adding a touch of white powder, heated it again until it turned dark blue, and then with another touch of white powder and more heat there was nothing in the crucible, no more liquid. The crucible was dry.

Maureen smiled.

Josh bowed a magician's bow.

Harrison said, "Ever think about the possibility of fire hazard?"

"I'm very careful," Josh said.

"A Bunsen burner gives intense heat."

"I know, and I'm careful believe me. But, Alan, you're giving me darn good advice, I realize that."

Alan, she thought. Twelve years old referring to thirty-five as Alan.

"Anything more?" Maureen asked.

"That's it for now." Josh yawned. "Excuse me," he said. "Getting sleepy. Good night, mother. Good night, Alan."

"Would you like a nightcap? Brandy?"

"I would indeed," Harrison said, and trailed her to the kitchen.

She had turned to go to the liquor cabinet when she saw the note attached by Scotch tape to the refrigerator, Laurie informing her that she and Diana hadn't wanted to disturb "you and Dr. Harrison" and so had gone off to bed without saying good-night.

"Our tom-tom system," Maureen said. "In this house, when we can't communicate verbally we do it by notes on the refrigerator door."

Sitting opposite each other at the kitchen table, they sipped brandy from large snifter glasses. "She calls you Dr. Harrison," Maureen said, "as you can see from her note." She took another sip of brandy and smiled, but it was forced. "Josh, it appears, now calls you Alan . . . would you like me to talk to him—?"

"Oh no, please don't inhibit him. I *am* Alan to him, just as he's Josh to me. We're friends. I've come to be very fond of that boy, and I think he feels the same about me."

She nodded briefly, said she was feeling pretty bushed herself and would have to excuse herself. She was sorry, hoped he didn't mind too much—

He kissed her. "Damn right, I mind. Maureen, I think it's past the time when—"

"No,"she said, more abruptly than she intended. She kissed him back, turned and went quickly upstairs to her room.

She fell asleep quickly . . . an escape from the thoughts about Josh that she had thought she'd succeeded in pushing down.

Ringing.

In the middle of the night.

It woke her. It did not, as she knew, wake anyone else.

She switched on the bed lamp, got out of bed and found a flashlight. With all the people in the house it would not do to click on the overhead lights in the middle of the night. She made her way to the attic and by flashlight found the little red phone, sank with it into the child's chair, put the receiver to her ear.

"Maury?"

Stop arguing with herself. Go along . . . "Yes," she said in the darkness in the middle of the night into a toy telephone.

The voice came over to her as if no time had elapsed. It seemed to pick up where it had left off . . . ". . . once it is completely formed it cannot be destroyed. First there has to be puberty and then, from its onset, a year is needed for it to become fully formed. Only during that year can it be destroyed. After one year it is too late. The year from onset of puberty, the year of incubation, also manifests an incubus that can perform acts of mesmerism in body-to-body contact.

"Remember, it is during this one year from the beginning of puberty that it can be destroyed. Maury, you have been given that work, the most important of your life—"

I must be crazy sitting here listening and answering, she thought, but she said, "What do you *want*? What important work . . . ?"

"Please be a little more patient, Maury. I have to prepare you first. It is only during the one year from puberty in-cubation period that it can be destroyed, and the only method is incineration. He can only be killed by fire. You will have to do it. You will have to kill what you know and think of as Josh—"

"*No*, stop it—"

But he did not stop it. "Maury, my time is running out. This will be my last chance to communicate with you . . . During the one year from puberty what represents itself as Josh must kill three times to obtain and drink fresh human blood, one pint or .473 liters each time. Don't ask me where this prescription came from, but I assure you it is accurate. The victims must be male human beings . . ." (A devilish chauvinism, she couldn't help thinking in the midst of this horrific recital.) ". . . and the killings must be spaced. Five months from the onset of puberty, then two months and then five months. Josh came to puberty in April. Five months later—September—he committed his first killing. Me—"

She tried to put down the receiver, to hang up, to turn away somehow and could not. All she could think of was her passing thought earlier that somehow Steve's murder was linked to the call on the little red telephone. Now she was hearing that what was only a farfetched notion in her head was more and more terribly close to home . . .

"It was Josh, Maury. He simply came up from behind me, cracked my head with a rock and cut my throat with his fishing knife. He's very adaptable, can quickly take advantage of any situation and make it plausibly seem the fault of someone else. He even managed to have you go off and leave him, with a mad killer presumably about, so that he could arrange things more convincingly." (Lord, she had done that, but it seemed necessary at the time, and it was hardly likely a killer would come back. He would have killed both of them, she'd reasoned, if he'd wanted to. Still . . .) "Now it is November, two months since my death. It will happen again, if it has not already—" (Chief Nolan, she thought, his throat was cut—)

He continued on, words coming faster, as though his time was indeed running out . . . "In five months, in April, he will make his final killing, unless you stop him. I will not call again. There will be no more ringing of a toy telephone to frighten you. I have no more time. Maury, I know how all this sounds to you. Remember, I was in your position before, except I did not have the opportunity to learn from Jack what I have since learned from him and now been able to pass on to you. Please, Maury, everything depends on you believing . . ."

And then dead silence.

It had been Steve's voice, abstracted and without its old vibrancy, but unmistakably his voice. But whose *words* were they? Was she in her delusions, linked with his, someone using events she knew about and giving them weird significance by making them seem to come from some damn ghostly, imagined voice? To convince herself that abnormal was normal, that the impossible was real? Two crazies, Steve and Maury, linked . . . ? And yet if she were crazy, how was it that she could function so well otherwise, make

171

meals, feel love for Alan . . . Don't be ridiculous, she lectured herself, of course everybody knows that the most crazy people can dissemble, can above all convince themselves that they are perfectly normal, and even act that way most of the time—

An abrupt noise pulled her from her thoughts. She looked up.

Josh was standing in the doorway. He flipped on the overhead light.

A blond boy in his undershorts, blinking sleep out of his eyes.

A blond woman seated, knees high, in a child's chair.

A blond boy squinting, as though unable to take in the bizarre scene in front of him—a blond woman in a child's chair talking into a toy telephone.

"I couldn't sleep, mom. Came downstairs for a glass of milk and thought I heard you talking up here . . . what's up, mom?"

"I guess you could call it mother getting old . . ."

He came toward her. He was smiling.

"I mean, you and Laurie are growing up . . . I suppose it's natural for a mother to think about when her children were babies . . . I came up here, started looking at all the old toys . . . this one, this little red phone, it was one of your favorites . . ."

"I know, mom, I remember. I still love it." He took the little phone out of her hands, seemed to fondle it. "I made calls all over the world on this phone. And when I got older, like nine or ten, I talked to Mars, Jupiter, Venus . . ." He put the receiver to his ear. "Hello?" he said. "Hello, Mars. Hello, Jupiter, Venus . . ." He laughed, replaced the receiver.

He carried the little red phone to its shelf and put it away. He walked about the room, looking at the shelves, then pulled down a battered copy of *Grimm's Fairy Tales*. "My favorite book," he said. "Remember? Me and Laurie, this one, 'Grimm,' we loved it. Remember we made you read to us over and over, from *Grimm's Fairy Tales*?"

"I remember," she said, fighting for control.

"How about now, mom?" He laughed, and handed her the book. "As long as you're in the mood, how about reading me a story just like you used to? How's about it, mom?"

"Don't you think you're a little too old for fairy tales?" (What a stupid thing to say.)

"Are you?"

"No," she said.

"Then how's about it, mom?"

He sat down, knees high, in a child's chair next to her. She smiled at him. He smiled back. "All right, here goes," she said as she willed her fingers to open the battered old copy of *Grimm's Fairy Tales*.

Twenty ∿∾

NOW WHAT?

Early December. Four months to go if—*cut it out Maureen*. But go see Dr. Sam. At least do that.

She complained to Alan of slight pains in her lower abdomen. He examined her by hand touch—pressure, palpation—found nothing. She refused further tests. "Not by you," she said. "The old story—the surgeon doesn't operate on his own, and we're too close. I don't want you to be my doctor, and I don't think you want to be my doctor."

He agreed. "Ron Harvey," he said. "He's a good man, a good doctor—"

"No. Time I went to New York for a check-up by a man who's been my internist for years, and also my gynecologist, Dr. Arnold Gordon. We won't tell any of this to the kids. We'll say I decided to go to New York for a day or two to do some Christmas shopping . . ."

She called Dr. Sam, told him she was coming to New York for a few days and requested a professional appointment. He insisted that she stay at his apartment. It was pre-Christmas in New York, its busiest time; the hotels were overcrowded and expensive. His apartment comprised eight rooms. "Three of those rooms do absolutely nothing, they're virtually guest rooms but I don't have any guests." She thanked him and accepted.

She flew out the second Tuesday in December and it was on the plane that she began changing her mind about

174

her planned confession to Dr. Samuel Vaughn. Even *he* would put her away if she told *all* of the stuff she'd heard. She would tell him about hearing the ringing, she would ask about this *folie à deux*, she might even let on that once she had imagined she'd heard Steve's voice on that toy telephone . . . aural hallucination within the syndrome of a *folie à deux?* She'd pump the good doctor, not only checking out her own brain but picking his . . .

New York was so beautiful, so ugly and so *tall*.

It was only six months but already she was a stranger, a foreigner reduced in size, a Lilliputian in the vast canyons of the city . . .

Dr. Sam's building, on Fifty-third east of Fifth, was another towering edifice blotting out the sky. The elevator, swiftly ascending to sixteen, stopped the breath in her throat and made her ears feel empty.

She rang the bell of 16-A and he opened quickly.

He embraced her, kissed her cheek, took her bag and led her to her room. "All yours," he said. "Wash up, rest, relax. When you get hungry, make coffee in the kitchen and take food." He looked at his watch. "Our session will be in a couple-three hours . . ."

Sitting opposite him in the consultation room, she remembered that when she was here last it was April.

April. The month of the twins' birthday.

April. The month the twins had come to puberty . . . April, the voice had said . . .

"You look a bit drawn," Dr. Sam was saying. "Are you all right?"

"Physically, yes. Otherwise, I'd say I've got a few problems."

"You've come to the right fix-it shop . . . How're the kids?"

"Fine."

"Dr. Harrison?"

"Fine."

He sat back, lit his pipe, waited.

She sat back and stared at him. April. A hundred years ago. Before Acheron Falls, and the big wooden house, and Alan Harrison, and Diana, and Essie Prichard, and Mitchell Ranson and Police Chief Marcus Nolan. Before the ringing in the attic—Jack Mercer to Steven Blair. Before the rape and murder of Clare Selwyn, before the murder of Steven Blair, before the murder of Marcus Nolan, before the ringing again of that damned little red phone . . .

"They don't know," she said, "the kids, nobody, that I'm here in New York specifically to see you. For the kids, I came for Christmas shopping. For Alan—Dr. Harrison—I faked some pains in the belly. He examined me superficially and of course found nothing. I told him I wanted my own internist and gynecologist in New York—Arnold Gordon—to check me out. I've no intention of seeing Arnold. I'm here to see you and, actually, to *do* some Christmas shopping. I'll be going back on Friday—"

"Specifically, what's it about?"

"Your *folie à deux*," she said. "That toy telephone began to ring—for *me*. For no one else. Just like with Steve. And once, I can swear I heard Steve's voice. Am I crazy, Dr. Sam? *Am* I?"

"You're not crazy. Please go on."

"That's it . . . except it's stopped now . . ."

"When did it start?"

"In October. A couple of times in October. And then in November."

"When did you hear his voice?"

"I imagined I heard it—"

"When?"

"Middle of November."

"How many times?"

"Once. Just once. But it's all over now."

"When was the last time?"

"The ringing? a little before Thanksgiving. And that was

176

the last. It's not going to ring again, I know it's not going to ring again."

He smiled. "That's good."

"What's good?"

"That you *know*. *Folie à deux* happens more often than people imagine. Especially between people who are close with one another . . . husband and wife, lovers. Happens most especially when such couples are intelligent and have fertile imaginations."

He leaned forward, his arms on the desk. His deep, resonant voice was comforting. "You are not crazy, Maureen. But if ever there was a candidate for *folie à deux*, you are it. If I'd have had the nerve I'd have predicted it—the *folie* of Maureen to follow precisely the pattern of Steve's *folie*, which is the way it happened . . . the same aural hallucination of the ringing phone and even your hearing a voice coming from that toy telephone. This thing with you is not major. Call it a little madness—an ordinary little madness—that cures itself. You're not crazy, dear Maureen. I'm an old soldier and I earned my stripes on the battlefield. A good long look, and I can see. I've looked at your face, your eyes, your facial expressions, your movements, the body language . . . you are not crazy . . ."

Was that good? Or bad? If she was not crazy, then what in the hell happened up there in the attic in the tall wooden house in Acheron Falls?

"When you say you know that toy telephone is not going to ring again, then there we have it." He reamed his pipe, packed it again, lit it and puffed. "The *folie* is of the imagination, and when the imagination closes it down—then it is over. *You* told *me*. You *know* that phone isn't going to ring again. Good. Once again nature has done the work that we therapists strive to do . . ." He puffed his pipe. "You'll be here till Friday? Well, I've made plans. Got to give you a taste of the Apple again. Tonight we'll eat in, I'll cook. Then we go to a movie, a preview of Francis Coppola's latest opus. Daytime, you're on your own. Do your shopping, visit with old friends. Nighttime, you're mine.

"Tomorrow night we dine at La Caravelle, then we go see an off-Broadway revival of *Death of a Salesman*. Thursday night, Lutece, then the Met for *Lucia di Lammermoor*. Friday you're on your own. I'll be flying out early morning to California where I'm to do three lectures at three universities."

He pointed an index finger, vertical. "Just a minute."

"I'm not going anywhere."

"Tension."

"What?"

"Tension, that's what you'll report back about your pain in the belly. It covers all manner of nonpathological psychosomatic ills. It used to be stress, now it's tension. Arnold Gordon checked you out, found you to be healthy, attributed your pain in the belly to pandemic tension. He told you to think positive and eat a lot of vitamin C and kelp if you can, and soon enough, if not sooner"—he laughed—"the knot in your stomach will dissolve and the pain will go away."

"Thank *you*, doctor."

"You are not crazy. Please fix that in your mind."

"Thank you, doctor."

"You're welcome. Now get out of here. I've got *sick* people coming."

It was a wonderful vacation in New York. Daytime she visited with old friends, nighttimes she was squired by her best friend, the rotund, wonderful Dr. Samuel Vaughn. She limited her shopping to Saks and Georg Jensen's. At Saks she did Christmas shopping for Laurie, Josh, Diana, Alan and Essie and arranged to have those purchases shipped out to Acheron Falls, not to arrive until after Friday. At Jensen's she bought small carry-home presents, and an exquisite silver-and-malachite ashtray for Dr. Sam.

On Friday she woke up early. Dr. Sam was already gone. She had breakfast in the kitchen, wrote a thank-you note and attached it with Scotch tape to the refrigerator. She took Dr. Sam's gift to his consultation room and put it in the center of his desk. She took the keys he'd left her, locked the apartment and gave the keys to the doorman.

She was early. It was hours before plane time.

She strolled down Fifth Avenue and there at Fiftieth Street—it was as if unconsciously she knew where she was going—loomed St. Patrick's Cathedral. She walked up the broad steps into the quiet, beautiful church. She sat in a back pew, alone. She sat there for a long time, silently praying to God.

Twenty-One ~ooo~

NO MORE ringing in the attic. At least Steve's voice and Dr. Sam were together on that.

She had come home on Friday bearing gifts. She had come home to Alan's house and rejoined her family. She had stayed the weekend; on Sunday they had had all gone fishing, even Essie, on Ron Harvey's wonderful boat. . . .

She submerged herself in work. Substitute teacher. Alan, chairman of the board of education, got her added as a sixth member. She had the academic training, she'd been a schoolteacher in New York City and she was the widow of a schoolteacher. They loved her in Acheron Falls.

As December passed into January, all the Blair weekends were spent with the Harrisons. Alan closed his office on Saturdays and Sundays—as did Dr. Ronald Harvey—and Dr. Lyndon Tucker, to whom they referred their emergency calls, had a weekend practice that swelled and everybody was happy, especially old Dr. Lyndon Tucker.

Weekends the Blairs and the Harrisons went skiing at Mt. Snow, staying over at the warm, commodious Mt. Snow Lodge. Often they split the weekend, going off on Friday to Mt. Snow, and coming home for Sunday fishing with Ron Harvey and his wife, Helen.

No more toy telephone ringing in the attic.

But now she apparently was punishing herself with dreams, and waking up aching with guilt about them. It was a dream she had first had . . . it seemed so long ago . . . in September when Steve was still alive. It was obscene. The partner in the dream was Josh, and now that dream was coming back, and when she woke up she remembered the sensation of orgasm . . .

Why was she doing this to herself?

Why this new means of self-punishment?

On this particular Saturday in January they did not go skiing on Mt. Snow but instead went fishing with the Harveys. "I was busy, it slipped my mind, I called too late for the reservation," Alan told her. "This time of year, you just can't do that. They might find room for one of us, but not four—"

"All right, please don't sound so apologetic," Maureen said.

The Harveys were glad.

So was Josh. "I don't want to hurt anybody's feelings," he said, looking at Alan, "but this weekend I'll take fishing over skiing. You been reading the papers? They say the cod are running like fifty pounds and up. That's *real* big fishing."

"A boy after my own heart," Ron Harvey said, and rubbed Josh's golden hair. He opened a paper. "Everybody dress real warm." He grinned, rubbed Josh's head again, then read from the paper: " 'Fishing and boating forecast, marine conditions: wind becoming northwest at fifteen to thirty knots. Seas: waves four to eight feet. Air temperature: low thirties. Water temperature: low thirties. Visibility: gradually diminishing from five miles. Possibility of freezing rain late afternoon.' That's real big-cod weather, folks. We can bring one in that'll break a record. But the least we'll do this day, I promise, is haul in enough lunkers to feed the poor of this town for a month. Just remember, everybody, dress warm."

A hot Maine sun quickly warmed the air, and the three who were fishing divested themselves of some of their outer clothing. The three at the stern were Ron, Alan and Josh, with Maureen watching. In the deckhouse at the wheel was

Helen Harvey, a skilled mariner; in the salon playing Scrabble were Diana and Laura, who had made it clear that they would have preferred to be skiing.

By two in the afternoon Dr. Ronald Harvey's prophecy had been fulfilled—except for a record breaker. Alan was high hook with twelve cod to fifty pounds; next was Josh with ten cod to fifty pounds; and last was Ron Harvey, who in numbers had nailed more than the others but his best catch was a thirty-seven-pounder. The haul was at forty-six cod when Ron Harvey called off the fishing because of a storm, sudden and unexpected, that blew in from the north. The weather bureau had predicted the possibility of freezing rain—but this was a dangerous winter storm.

The sky grew black.

Helen Harvey put on the boat's lights.

"You guys pull in all the paraphernalia," Ron Harvey ordered as the slanting wind-driven rain lashed at them. "I'll be up in the deckhouse."

Maureen stayed, trying to help. They drew up all manner of clanking material and pulled them to places of safety out of the wind.

Alan was hurrying again toward the stern when he tripped over a coil of rope and fell forward; his head struck the edge of the deck, and he tumbled overboard. Immediately Josh tore out of his coat, kicked off his loafers and plunged into the roiling sea.

Maureen ran to the deckhouse, to Ron Harvey at the wheel. "They're *overboard*. Both of them, Alan fell and Josh went in after him—"

"Turn on the spotlight," Harvey yelled to his wife. Helen Harvey switched on the powerful searchlight. "Now hang on, you two," he shouted against the noise of the wind. "I'm circling all the way, one hundred and eighty degrees." His eyes went to Maureen. They'd been heading home at a good speed, there already must be a hell of a lot of distance between the boat and the two in the water . . . "Helen, keep sweeping that spotlight over the water. Maureen, go forward. Yell if you spot them."

Maureen ran.

"Not good," Harvey muttered to himself. The Coast Guard had reported a thirty-three degree water temperature. One degree above freezing. Those two weren't going to last long in that kind of water . . . He reached for the radio mike and called the Coast Guard to have an ambulance waiting at the marina . . .

The boat circled the area in an ever-widening orbit; when it became too wide Harvey circled back slowly, inward. A harrowing twenty minutes passed. And then Helen's searchlight caught the two men entwined in the black sea. Actually they were quite near the boat . . . Maureen could see that Josh was the swimmer, treading water, holding up a limp Alan Harrison.

Harvey came running down from the deckhouse, threw a line and then lifejackets to the two figures embraced within the dead white cincture of Helen Harvey's spotlight. The lifejackets floated away, but Josh managed to catch the line and held it until Harvey pulled them in.

Helen shone the spotlight down on the deck.

Alan's eyes were closed, his face blue, his lips white. He did not seem to be breathing. Josh looked just as bad, but he was breathing, his lips moved. He was mumbling.

The girls were there, Diana and Laura, ready to help.

"All right now," Harvey said, "you and I, Diana, will take Alan to the master stateroom. Maureen, you and Laura get Josh into the forward stateroom. Take his clothes off and wrap him in blankets. Keep him *warm*, warm as possible. I'll come to you soon as I can. Alan is first, he's in the worst shape . . ."

In the master stateroom Harvey stripped off Alan's wet clothes and wrapped him in blankets. "Lie near him," he told Diana. "He needs body warmth."

He went off and quickly came back with his medical bag,

183

which he always kept on board. He listened with his stethescope to Alan's chest. "He's alive, barely. No sense me trying to fool anybody." He filled a hypodermic, pulled away a blanket, injected Alan Harrison's left arm. "A stimulant," he said. He replaced the blanket, inserted a thermometer between Alan's lips. When he drew it out he looked pale. Ninety-one-point-one. Normal body temperature was ninety-eight-point-six . . . he hurried off to see Josh.

In the forward stateroom Josh was sprawled on his back under blankets, but his eyes were open. His heart was "thumping pretty good," Harvey told Maureen and Laura, but his temperature was only one degree higher than Alan's. He filled the hypodermic again and injected Josh. Go by the book, he told himself, even if he doubted it would do much good. Josh was in better shape . . . he couldn't speak and didn't react to proddings but his eyes were open, blinking, and his heart sounds were better than Alan's. Alan was comatose, had a fluttering heartbeat. Either one of them could die unless they got to a hospital on time . . . .

In the master stateroom Alan lay wrapped in blankets, Diana near with an arm lightly about him. His eyes were closed, but Maureen could see that at least he was breathing. She pointed to a lump on his forehead.

Ron Harvey shrugged. "That's the least of our troubles. Probably where he hit his head when he stumbled and went overboard. Our problem is hypothermia." He slid the thermometer into Alan's mouth again.

"What's hypothermia?"

"It means loss of body heat . . . Diana, it's okay, why don't you go to Laura? She's all alone in the forward stateroom with Josh. She may need you . . . we'll hold the fort here . . ."

Diana looked to Maureen.

"I'll be right here with your dad," Maureen said.

Diana got up from the bed, looking as terrified as she felt, and ran out of the room.

"That was good of you," Maureen said. "Twelve years

old—that's too young to watch your father . . . maybe dying . . ." Maureen nearly choked on the word.

Harvey took the thermometer from Harrison's mouth. "Ninety-one-point-six." A slight improvement, but still way below normal.

"Hypothermia, doctor?"

"Excuse me," he said. "I need to go up and check with Helen." He smiled bleakly. "Right now she's the captain of this ship."

When he returned he found Maureen lying close to Alan. "Not really necessary anymore," he said. "The layers of blankets are holding in his body heat now."

She moved down to the foot of the bed.

He bent to Alan, felt his forehead, listened by ear through the blankets to Alan's heart. "Helen says we're fifteen minutes from shore and there's an ambulance with paramedics waiting for us at the marina."

"In the meantime can't we do better than just blankets? Can't we put him into a hot bath?"

"It won't help."

"Why not?"

"This is hypothermia induced by freezing water. You've heard of people abandoned in the cold who freeze to death? The cause of that kind of death is hypothermia, but it works slowly. Even rescued hours later, many such people can be resuscitated. I'm afraid freezing water is a different story. It sucks the warmth out of a person's body many times faster than air at the same temperature."

"Then why don't we put him and Josh into a hot bath—?" Her voice, not surprisingly, held an edge.

"Putting a person in a hot tub can do more harm than good. It dilates the blood vessels but it does nothing to warm the organs at the body's core."

"Then what in God's name do we *do*?"

"What we *are* doing, Maureen. I know it's hard for you

185

to accept, but until we get them to a hospital where they can gradually raise the inner-core temperature . . . well, there's nothing more we can do—"

At which point, incredibly, impossibly, Josh walked into the stateroom.

Dr. Harvey could not speak.

Behind Josh and on either side of him stood Laura and Diana.

"We couldn't hold him back," Laura said, shaking her head. "He just got up and got some clothes from Dr. Harvey's closet . . ."

Josh smiled at Maureen, his pale blue eyes seemingly amused.

Harvey went to the boy, touched his face, pulled down his lower lids and peered into his eyes. He took his pulse. "I don't *believe* this," he said. "I don't believe—"

"How's Alan?" Josh asked.

Harvey could only point to the man wrapped in blankets on the bed. Again he put his hands on the boy's face, again took his pulse. "Hypothermia . . . freezing water . . . twenty minutes . . . there can't be this fast a recovery from hypothermia—"

"But there can be," Josh said proudly, "because here I am."

"Well, all I can say is, this is one for the books. I guess it can happen because it *has* happened, you're proof of it, Josh, but I still can't accept it. It's impossible, incredible. Lord, it's unreal, it's *unnatural* . . ."

Twenty-Two ∞∞

Unnatural.

A short trip from there to *supernatural*?

A chink in her armor of rationalization? True, Ron Harvey had also said, "In my business, if you've been at it long enough, if you've been around the track a few times, and I have been, well, you do begin to believe at least in the possibility of miracles. We've seen spontaneous remissions from apparently terminal cancer. So why not Josh's spontaneous remission from mere hypothermia . . ."

Except he hadn't sounded very convincing.

At the marina Alan had been carried to the ambulance on a stretcher, but Josh had walked off under his own power and refused any aid.

"I'm okay, I'm all right," he had said, but Dr. Harvey insisted Josh stay at the hospital for at least a day, and Maureen had stayed with him. In the morning, Josh had been discharged and the doctors, in obvious wonderment, had not talked about miracles. They had talked about the marvels of spontaneous remission.

Alan stayed in treatment in the hospital for three days, then on Wednesday he was discharged with a clean bill of health. He had been lucky, they said. A few more minutes in that freezing water and it would have been all over. In fact, he probably would have drowned if it had not been for Josh diving in and holding him up.

Maureen could not get over Dr. Harvey's talk about the

unnatural . . . something he simply couldn't explain for all his traditional, scientific training. So who was she to fight it so hard? Where do we start?

With the little red phone in the attic. But I must go all the way. I must believe that Steve heard the ringing and heard the voice of Jack Mercer. And then I must accept that I heard the ringing and heard Steve's voice, and I must believe what Steve had told me . . . that Joshua Mercer Blair is an evil force that has to be destroyed by fire within his first year of puberty . . . that he will kill three times for human blood . . . a male's . . . that he first killed in September and then in November and the third time will be in April. I have until the end of March . . .

Steve's death had been attributed to Mitch Ranson, but Marcus Nolan's murder never been solved. And it had happened in November—the second month in the five-two-five formula . . . It would have been easy. Everybody knew there was a person alone in the station house from midnight until eight in the morning. Chief Nolan had been killed on a Saturday night, and that night the Blairs had been sleeping over at the Harrison house, and Josh slept downstairs in the living room. He could have gotten up at midnight, dressed and slipped out of the house with one of Steve's fishing knives . . . He walks to the station house, finds Nolan there alone, as expected. He tells about not being able to sleep and going out for a walk, and flatters the old man about how glad he is to find him on duty because he knows the chief likes him and he admires the chief . . . how easy to maneuver himself behind the chief . . . He gets rid of the knife—in the sea—and goes back to the Harrison house . . . Alan had been awakened at one o'clock by a phone call from Dan Corely and hadn't returned until five Sunday morning. If there had been any bloodstains on Josh's clothes he'd have had the time to wash them out and there'd even been time for them to dry—

But if Josh was so malevolent, why did he dive in to save

Alan when he tripped, hit his head and tumbled overboard?

The answer came with a terrifying logic . . . reason within unreason, rational within irrational. Josh did not want to lose him because he was his long-intended third and final victim. And by what seemed a selfless act he had also insured that come April, when it would be time, Alan would be thoroughly unsuspecting. And now she remembered how carefully Josh had cultivated his friendship with Alan, how he—

Enough.

But she could not shut it out.

The dreams became more frequent, more vivid.

Perhaps by thinking the unthinkable, she had unleashed her own inner demons. Obscene intercourse with her son, a twelve-year-old boy. And they went on night after night.

Self-punishment for her thoughts about him?

Her own building sexual need? For Alan . . . Alan, her future lover and husband, she hoped. Alan, Josh's third victim . . . Did it somehow fit . . . ?

And then one afternoon the last of Steve's warnings surfaced, took shape. She remembered too clearly, a Sunday in November before Thanksgiving. Alan, Diana, Essie had been there for a fish dinner, and then in the middle of the night the ringing in the attic and Steve's voice telling her that the year from the onset of puberty was its year of incubation *and* that during that year there would be an incubus that could perform acts of mesmerism in body-to-body contact . . .

Incubation . . . Incubus. Sound-alikes. In her fright and disbelief she had run the two words and their meanings together. Incubus . . . she'd heard the word but didn't really know its meaning. She hurried up to the study, got out a dictionary.

> in-cu-bus (*in-kyoo-bes*), n. a demon supposed to descend
> upon sleeping persons, esp. one in male form fabled to
> have sexual intercourse with women in their sleep.

189

She closed the book and held tightly onto it, as if for support. She bit down on her lower lip, needing the reality of physical pain, and felt the taste of blood in her mouth. Acts of mesmerism in body-to-body contact . . . If so, then the dreams had not been dreams at all . . . they had been *real*. He . . . it . . . had gotten into bed with her, opened her legs and entered her . . . Josh, a twelve-year-old Josh—
No . . .

Think the unthinkable, you unhinge the floodgates. To hell with Ron Harvey and his talk about the unnatural and her own leap from there to accepting the reality of the unreal. Better the other way, Dr. Sam's small madness of the imagination that the imagination would shut down. An *ordinary* little madness like hers, he'd said, cures itself. The little red phone *had* stopped ringing, after all. Dr. Sam was the expert and he had said that *she* had turned it off. True, she hadn't told him everything, but she had told him enough to take advantage of his findings. The *folie* was dissipating, and soon it would end . . .

But it did not end.

The old station wagon was limping and even the town mechanic advised her to go see Rick Perry in Jackson City, "the best damn auto mechanic in the whole damn state of Maine." But she evaded it, and snapped at Josh when he said, "Mother, why in the heck *don't* you go see Rick in Jackson?" His beautiful, innocent eyes teared at her, "And why in *heck*, young man, don't you mind your own business?"

After all, Jackson City was a ninety-mile round trip and she just couldn't spare the time, what with all her duties at home and on the school board . . . She'd save Jackson City for late spring, when things got less hectic, less crazy . . .

It did not end.

They no longer went fishing on Ron Harvey's boat. "I

admit I'm superstitious," she said to Alan, "but the last time I saw you on Ron's boat you looked like a dead man. And according to Dr. Harvey you damn near were."

Josh, she noted . . . couldn't help but note . . . was especially unhappy about no more fishing with Alan and Dr. Harvey on the doctor's graceful forty-foot double-cabin cruiser.

It did not end.

In that month of January, she missed her period. Easy to explain, she quickly tried to assure herself, an accumulation that could disrupt any woman's system—the awful events on Ron Harvey's boat that day of the storm . . . the impact of the imagined ringing of that damned little red phone up there in the attic . . . the momentary acceptance of the voice on the phone and its wild talk about Josh and killings and an incubus, that last no doubt induced by her ever-increasing and *natural* sexual desire for the lover who so obviously also desired her . . .

Oh yes, so many reasons to explain the skipped menstrual period. And she clung, like a drowning woman, to them all. Until she was obliged to allow into her consciousness the most common and obvious reason for a woman missing her period—pregnancy. Never mind her fear, terror, she was Maureen Kirby Blair of Washburn, Bayfield County, Wisconsin, and she'd better not turn her mind away from *anything*, any possibility. If she *was* pregnant . . . put out of your mind how . . . then she'd damn well better commence a painfully delayed relationship with Alan Harrison. She'd know soon enough if she were truly pregnant, and if so she would marry Alan, and be glad of it, and their baby would be legitimate . . .

She would not have an abortion. She had been reared strictly as a Roman Catholic, and although she had broken away from much of the dogma, certain of the basic precepts had been annealed into her soul. If there *was* a child growing

191

in her uterus, even if it were that incubus . . . well, who was to say the child should suffer . . . if Josh were what Steve's voice had claimed, Laura, his twin, was not . . .

On Saturday she had allowed—arranged—an outing at Mt. Snow, where all of them were present except Josh, who stayed at home doing his chemistry, perhaps still sulking about her cutting off the fishing with Alan on Ron Harvey's boat. It was a perfect day, the snow was perfect, and the girls kept at it until near exhaustion, so that by nine o'clock they were sound asleep.

At ten Maureen and Alan in their separate rooms changed into evening dress and rendezvoused later in the nightclub of the Mt. Snow Lodge. They drank champagne, danced. Maureen gradually moved closer into Alan's arms. He looked down at her smooth bare shoulders, and beyond.

Was she finally coming around . . . ?

And as if reading his mind . . . not so difficult . . . she said, "In case you're wondering, doctor, the answer is yes . . ."

Upstairs in his room at first they were both understandably, nervous. But their mutual desire quickly overcame that, submerged all questions Alan might have had about why she had finally decided to allow this. Her beauty, the loving relief and fulfillment for both of them were all that existed.

Nor was there any exchange about contraception. Alan wanted nothing more than to marry her, to father her child. He had already been delighted to assume the role of surrogate father with Josh.

Actually she had prepared herself and would continue to do so whenever they would be together. If she were not pregnant, she did not want to create a situation to pressure him . . . But if she were pregnant, then Alan would think himself the father. Even knowing she had used a contraceptive . . . and she was not proud of herself for such thinking, however necessary she felt it was . . . he could not be certain

192

that the child was not his. No contraceptive, as doctors were quick to remind people, was infallible . . .

But all such thinking had been on her mind before this night. For these wonderful few hours, there was nothing of importance except their love . . .

Twenty-Three ~∞∞∞

THE RESPITE was short-lived.

On Thursday Laura complained of a severe headache and stomach cramps. Maureen quickly drove Josh to school, dropped him off, turned the car around and sped home as quickly as the bad roads would allow . . . to find Laura in the kitchen eating heartily of bacon and eggs *and* French-fried potatoes.

"This is sick?" Maureen said.

Laura said, "I'm not sick."

"No headache? No bellyache?"

"No."

"Then what?"

The child kept her eyes down, continued to eat her bacon and eggs.

Maureen sat down at the kitchen table. She stole a piece of bacon and nibbled. She smiled sympathetically. "Look, it's no crime for anybody to want a day off from school. But you just could have told me. I mean, your way, the way you did it, well . . . you had me scared."

"I would have told you, but that's not it. Not a day off from school . . ."

"Then *what*?"

Laura was silent.

Maureen's heart began to thump.

The breakfast was finished. Laura laid the fork on the plate and pushed it away. But her eyes remained down. "It's well, I . . . I wanted to talk to you, but alone . . . just you and me . . ."

"Sure, honey, that's what mothers are for—to talk to."

Laura looked up. There was no fear in her large blue eyes, more, it seemed, a puzzlement. "Not yet and not here," Laura said. "Later, in my room. Let's just do the dishes now, okay? But no dishwasher. Let's do them like you told me your mother used to do them, by hand so she could see with her own eyes that every dish was spic-and-span . . ."

Maureen understood. Laurie was stalling for time.

"Okay, kiddo," she said. "You wash, I dry."

It was the pleasantest room in the house, all the way to the south and at the furthest extreme from Josh's room. His bedroom at the northwest corner and directly above the garage was the largest room, serving him both as bedroom and laboratory. Laurie's exposure, southwest, always suffused her room with a warm soft light; the large window faced the front of the house, the west, and the smaller window faced the south. It was also the prettiest room, feminine and done in pastel shades.

Now Laurie was sitting knees up on the edge of a hassock, and Maureen, legs outstretched and hands folded on her stomach, lounged in a sturdy pink-and-yellow wing chair.

"What I'm going to tell you may sound crazy," Laurie said.

"Psychiatrists get paid for listening. Mothers do it for free." Was her little girl in love? First love could be shattering . . . she remembered her own first in Washburn, Wisconsin, when she had fallen in love with her schoolteacher, who also happened to be her father's friend and was even older than her father . . .

"It's about a dream I keep having," Laurie said. "A *crazy* dream."

Maureen pulled in her legs and sat up in the wing chair. The thumping in her chest returned, more violent than before. "A dream?" she managed to say, mildly, and tried to smile.

"More a nightmare, but it keeps on happening . . . it happened again the night we got home from Mt. Snow—and that's when I made up my mind I should talk to you about it—"

"We got home on Sunday. Today's Thursday."

"It's . . . well . . . not very easy to talk about, and I kept postponing, but today . . . well . . . that's why I said I was sick this morning, so you could come right back after you took Josh to school and we'd be alone . . ."

"I'm here, love, and we're alone."

There were tears in Laura's eyes. "Oh God, mom, I'm so embarrassed I want to die . . ."

Maureen said nothing, holding her breath, waiting.

"It's a . . . dirty dream . . . an awful dream—"

Maureen broke in. "Just tell your mother about those dirty awful dreams." She forced herself to smile, but felt sick to her stomach.

Laura hugged her knees and began to rock on the hassock. "Josh," she said abruptly, almost spitting out the name. "The dreams are about Josh . . ."

Maureen wanted to scream, clenched her teeth.

Laura spoke so softly now that Maureen had to strain to hear. "The first time was about a month after daddy died. I had my period . . . it was the first day . . . Well, anyway, in the dream it's nighttime and I'm asleep and . . . Josh comes into my room. No clothes on. He gets into my bed and he . . . he takes off my pad and . . . you know . . . he does it to me. Then he puts back the pad and goes away. That dream happened four nights in a row, the four days of my period." She stopped rocking on the hassock, looked up at her mother. "Since then I get that same dream a few times every month, not during my period. The last time was Sunday . . ."

Silence. The daughter looking at her mother. The mother trying to unlock herself from her own nightmare. Finally

196

Maureen smiled. Her hands, like released claws, became detached from the wing chair. "Laurie, I'm no expert but I can tell you that a recurring nightmare is nothing unusual. I've had a few myself. Yours, of course, is upsetting. After all it involves your own brother . . . but, honey, that's not so unusual either. I know, this may shock you, but psychiatrists tell us that brothers and sisters often have sexual fantasies about each other. And naturally it's so upsetting that most people never mention it, which can be dangerous because it can make for all sorts of unnecessary guilts. That's why I'm so glad you've told me about this. I'm grateful you trust me and can talk to me. Now don't you worry, honey, we'll handle this, just like we've handled all our other problems. Okay . . . ?"

"Okay . . . I love you, mom," and she hugged her mother as though she would never let her go.

"And I love you, baby. Don't you ever forget it."

With Laurie ensconced in her sunny room, Maureen went to the study. No more stalling . . . It was time. She had held back. She had closed the doors of her mind. Time now to open them.

Coincidence? How far can you go claiming coincidence?

Coincidence that the mother dreams that the son has sex with her, and the daughter dreams that he is having sex with *her*? She shuddered. A little normal nuttiness runs out as protection . . . and the unacceptable facts, reality, finally intrudes. Demands attention. Demands action. To avoid it any longer would indeed be madness.

Oh, she fought it, even now she fought it. But face it . . . how damnably . . . she almost thought devilishly and rejected the word . . . clever of him . . . Laura was a virgin. Mesmerized, she would not feel the pain of the rupture of the hymen, but there would be telltale blood. So he, the incubus . . . or whatever the hell it was . . . had done it the first time during her period.

Act. There were tests that could not be denied. If they

turned out negative, then Josh was Josh, a bright beautiful boy, and something peculiar beyond comprehension had been playing ugly perverse jokes on Maureen Blair. But if they were positive . . . then there was work to be done. Get the hell on with it.

She called New York and got through to Dr. Arnold Gordon, who offered his condolences.

She remembered. Arnie Gordon had been on her obituary list and Dr. Sam had sent him an announcement card of Steve's death. "Thank you," she said, and then, "I'd like to come in for a checkup. And Laurie with me. Same deal. Checkup."

He was her doctor and a friend, and he detected a note of urgency. "Is something wrong?"

"No, not really."

"Hold on a moment." She knew he was running a finger down along his appointment book. "Next Saturday," he said. "The Saturday after this one. One o'clock. Is that okay for you?"

"Yes. We'll be coming in on Friday, for a weekend of shopping. I'd prefer Laurie not know that I want her to have a thorough internal."

"Then there is something wrong . . ."

"Don't press me, Arnie. Not now. It's important for both of us—I mean Laurie and me. And, please, another thing. I was in New York in December and Dr. Sam insisted that I stay at his place. If he knows we're coming to New York next weekend he'll insist again. You know me—I just can't impose like that. So, if you don't mind, two things. Don't mention to Dr. Sam that we're coming to town and can you recommend a quiet hotel for us."

"Yes and yes. The hotel is the Wyndham, and it's right here on my street." Dr. Arnold Gordon's office was on Fifty-eighth between Fifth and Sixth. "The Wyndham, Forty-two West Fifty-eighth. You'll like it. Friday, Saturday,

198

Sunday. I'll take care of the reservations. Good-bye now, see you Saturday after this Saturday. One o'clock."

She went to Laurie's sunny room, and this time she sat on the hassock. "I've dreamed us up a little vacation. We both could use it. Change of scenery. A little vacation and a lot of shopping. A weekend in New York City. How's that hit you?"

"Sounds super," Laurie said.

Maureen stood up. She smiled. "I've been having some nightmares too. We've been through a lot—all of us—since daddy. And I'm fitting in some health business—"

"Health business?"

"I called Dr. Gordon. Time for my annual checkup. And for you too, young lady . . . you're a woman now. You won't lose too much time from school. We'll have our shopping spree the weekend after this and in between, on Saturday, we'll drop in on Doc Gordon for our checkups. But don't mention the checkup business to anyone—not Josh, Diana or even Dr. Harrison. These are women's matters, personal matters . . . Just you and me, honey. Okay?"

Josh accepted being left behind, but said brightly that since he was being so nice and cooperative, she had to allow him to go fishing. "Dr. Harvey keeps asking us and we keep refusing—even with Alan along—because you won't let us. How about it?"

She let him, because she could no longer think of a reason to forbid it without somehow tipping her hand. They'd all have to take chances . . .

"But the weather must be good," she said, trying to recoup a little.

"I will promise you that," Alan said.

"It'll be our last chance for a long time," Josh said. "After that Dr. Harvey's going south for a month's vacation."

"But *only* if the weather's right," Maureen said, feeling weak in her stomach.

"Sure. And I'll stay for the weekend at Alan's house," Josh said quietly, smiling at her.

Lying in bed that night, Maureen thought for a moment of Diana and Essie, in the same house as him . . . But Diana was still prepubescent so he wouldn't risk anything with her, and Essie was a self-proclaimed virgin . . . at her age, what else to do but flaunt it . . . ?

Damn it, *no*. No more thinking. This trip would settle it, and then they'd all be back to normal, everything would be the way it used to be.

Sleep, Maureen, or you'll really go crazy.

New York this time of year was cold, brisk, clear and even clean; and the Wyndham Hotel turned out to be as comfortable as Dr. Gordon had said. On Friday they went from store to store shopping, most of it for Laurie. On her own Maureen made certain to buy two small wide-mouthed bottles with secure turn-on tops and a roll of white one-inch adhesive tape. She did not purchase a ball-point pen because in her handbag, buried beneath the detritus contained in all women's handbags, there lurked somewhere down there a perfectly seviceable ball-point pen. They had lunch in a good restaurant, and later they had dinner in a great restaurant, and then went to see a play.

On Saturday they did not get out of bed until nine o'clock, and when Laurie was about to go in for her shower Maureen gave her one of the wide-mouthed bottles. "For you to pee in, honey. You'll find it quite an acrobatic trick, but you'll manage. The men don't know how easy they have it. When you're done close it up with that screw-top cap. Okay? And then it'll be my turn."

She knew they'd take urine samples as a matter of course at the doctor's, but this way, using absolutely pristene bottles, there would be no possible chance of a mix-up. These tests had to be beyond chance . . .

When Laurie closed the bathroom door Maureen went to the phone and called Dr. Arnold Gordon. "Just confirming," she said. "Today, one o'clock."

"Yes. You could have told my receptionist, Maureen. I am rather busy—"

"But I have to talk to *you*. It's something that I should have told you. Please be sure you take me first. Get me into the examination room where I can be alone with you. There are things I must tell you about Laurie. She won't tell you and she'd be mortified if she knew I told you . . ."

Lies. But necessary.

"I understand. Sorry I was abrupt with you."

"See you at one o'clock, doctor."

Dr. Arnold Gordon's office was on Fifty-eighth Street on the ground floor, street level. At one o'clock sharp Maureen, with Laura, rang his bell.

The waiting room was large and tastefully furnished, with a receptionist seated behind a small neat desk. Beyond was the doctor's consultation room, an adjacent private waiting room and three spotless white examination rooms, each with a contiguous dressing room. In the rear was a lab and a lab technician. These were the offices of one of the most respected and successful internist-gynecologists in New York City. Maureen had met him through Steve during the first year of their marriage, and he had become one of their circle, a friend. Even back then Arnie Gordon's reputation was growing, he was on his way up; at that time his offices were three small rooms on the fourth floor of a tall building on lower Fifth Avenue.

The waiting room was empty, as it should be: Arnie Gordon was the same man he had always been, precise and considerate—and not greedy. He spaced his appointments with regard to the need of the patient and the time the patient required. In Dr. Arnold Gordon's office there was never a backlog of patients impatiently waiting in a crowded waiting room.

"I'm Mrs. Blair and this is my daughter," Maureen said to the receptionist.

"Yes. Doctor's expecting you." The receptionist opened a door for them, let them through and closed it behind them.

Smiling, Arnold Gordon stood up from his desk, kissed Maureen and Laura. "Sit down, ladies."

He was tall, a little gloomy-looking and very thin. He had black hair combed in a sweep from one side of his head to the other to cover his encroaching baldness. He had large, sorrowful brown eyes, but as though in counterbalance his black eyebrows were aggressively bushy. After some badinage Dr. Gordon smiled at Laura and said, "Well, time's wasting. It's a close decision, but as they say, age before beauty." He led Laura to a small private waiting room. "We won't be long. I'll do a quick check on your mama, and then you, and that'll be it . . ."

In the white examination room Maureen hugged him. "You were great. Maybe you missed your profession, maybe you should have been an actor."

"Well, you told me to be sure I took you first, that you wanted to be alone with me, things you had to tell me about Laura. You sounded pretty serious."

"I was. I am. But first I'll tell you something about me . . . It's possible . . . I don't really think I am . . . but it's possible that I'm pregnant."

His voice was flat, professional. "How long?"

"I've missed one period. Here's a urine specimen. Laurie has one too—"

"Maureen, we have facilities here—"

"I know, I know," and then she told him how she wanted to be sure no possible mistake was made, a mix-up of specimens.

He shrugged. Obviously she was very upset. "We'll also take some blood. It's too early for any pathology to show
202

in the internal, but from the blood tests and the urine I'll be able to tell you quite definitely."

"How soon?"

"I'll call you at your hotel. Six o'clock."

She got herself onto the examination table and prepared herself to tell lies to an old friend. "About Laurie," she said. It's a pretty strange story. It's one of those small-town tales people hear about but hardly ever believe." Suddenly her eyes were hard, defensive. "Don't *ever* tell her—don't ever even admit that you know what I'm about to tell you. Matter of fact, I doubt she knows that I've heard about it—"

"You can depend on me and you damn well know it."

"I know. I'm sorry. It's just—well, I'm, frightened, upset, as you can plainly see . . . Anyway, there was this boy in Acheron Falls. He had, as they say, a way with young girls . . . what do they call it? Animal magnetism. Listen, I don't know exactly when or how, but he seemed to have his way with young girls . . . twelve-thirteen-fourteen— and I'm sorry to say, it seems Laurie was a part of it. Why? God, who knows? No father . . . too much mother . . . anyway, this little creep—"

"Okay, Maureen. I get the picture. Relax. It's not the end of the world." He helped her off the examination table. "I think I know what you want. I'm the doctor, like they say . . . All right, let's please get on with you." He pointed to the dressing room. "You'll find a sealed package with a sterile gown. Get undressed and get into the gown and don't forget it goes on bass-ackward . . ."

They returned to the consultation room, where Dr. Gordon left her, seated at his desk. He then went for Laura and escorted her to another examination room, where a young nurse waited for them. He pointed. "That's the dressing room," he said. "You'll find a sterile package in there with a gown and towels. If you need any help or anything explained, Miss Mallory will be right outside the door. Any questions?"

203

"No," Laura said.

"Only thing that might be unpleasant . . . we'll take a bit of blood from your arm. I promise it won't hurt . . ."

Fifteen minutes later the doctor was back in the consultation room. "She's getting dressed," he said to Maureen, and sat in his chair facing her. "The hymen is ruptured. Of course it could be from some strenuous activity . . ." Maureen only looked at him, and when she did not speak—she couldn't— he went on. "In any case, I think it would be wise to have a pregnancy test for Laurie as well as for you. Of course it's up to you, but if she is pregnant, then I would recommend—and I know your beliefs—a therapeutic abortion. I don't believe that a twelve- or thirteen-year-old girl is emotionally ready to bear a child and be a mother . . ."

They left the doctor's office, mother and daughter, strolling arm in arm. "We have to be back at the hotel by six," Maureen said. "That's when Dr. Gordon'll call to give us the final word. So far it seems we're a couple of very healthy people."

Laura laughed. "Yes, that's what he told me too."

"Let's go in somewhere for a couple of quick hamburgers, then shop, and then when we get back to the Wyndham we can have them send up a great big whopping dinner."

Maureen squeezed her daughter's arm. "Honey, you look great. I think this is just what you needed. A vacation, a change of scenery—away from everybody. Just you and this here old mama bear having fun in the Big Apple. And for tomorrow I'm planning for a real getaway day. We'll have lunch at the Four Seasons, and then a last assault on the stores and then the show at Radio City Music Hall . . ."

At five-thirty they returned to their suite at the Wyndham Hotel. Maureen struggled out of her coat and dropped it on a chair. "I'm exhausted," she said.

"I'm starved," Laura said.

"I'm exhausted *and* starved."

They showered, changed to lounge clothes and Maureen called room service and ordered dinner.

The phone rang. Maureen looked at her watch. "Exactly six o'clock," she said. "He's the most meticulous man, our Dr. Gordon." She lifted the handset from its cradle, but made certain the receiver was pressed close to her ear. "Hello?"

"Maureen?"

"Yes."

Laurie was looking at her, and Maureen put on a smile. "It's me, doc. How're we doing, the Blair women . . . ?"

"Laurie is not pregnant," he said. "But you are."

"I see," Laurie was still looking at her, and so she still smiled, fixedly.

"Now listen to me. If you're willing to terminate this pregnancy, it's a very simple matter—"

"That's great . . . well, I'm afraid I have to go now. Our dinner is on its way. 'Bye, doc. And thanks." She hung up before he could answer and turned to Laurie.

"Well, honey, that's that, the results of the lab tests, and they couldn't be better. We're strong as a couple of bulls. Oh dear, that sounds wrong for women. Well, we're healthy as horses. We are—"

There was a knock on the door.

"Yes?" Maureen called.

"Room service," the man said.

Thank God, she thought.

Twenty-Four ~∞∞∞

BUT YOU cannot live on the momentary respite of room service, Maureen instructed herself, with something approaching a wry shrug, about her maximum achievement in humor these days.

Laura was a lovely but also rather sedentary child. She had never been much for even bike riding, and horses were something she preferred on TV. She did ski but was cautious on gentle slopes. Which tended to reinforce Maureen's conviction that her ruptured hymen did not occur in any of the sometime popular ways having nothing to do with sexual intercourse.

Now, though, with proof that *she* was pregnant, there was no point in worrying about Laura's situation. There was just no denying that *he* . . . she still found it almost impossible to use the name Josh in connection with what had been visited on her, on all of them . . . had indeed been the presence in her dream. She was carrying his child.

She barely made it through the weeks until March, going throught the motions of her daily duties, avoiding any outings and frequently even Alan, pleading kind of a renewed depression after going to New York and seeing an old friend like Arnold Gordon, a friend of Steve's, that brought back the shock of Steve's death and the memories. Alan, of course, didn't like it but went along . . . She thought about abortion, but rejected it. It would have been possible, despite her Catholic upbringing, if there were some way in which she could be positive that the unborn infant would be in its father's image, but of course there was no way to be sure of that . . . Josh and Laura proved that . . . the one so lovely and normal, the other . . .

Soon, though, she would have to talk to Alan, tell him, deceive him about the fact of her pregnancy. Time was drawing short. For that. And for the other, the most terrible act.

She remembered that Steve had said "He can only be killed by fire." Maureen, raised on, steeped in the Bible from childhood, finally allowed herself to remember her Catholic Bible. Matthew . . . 25:40 . . . Jesus saying . . . She went to her Bible, and yes, there it was, she was almost right . . . not 25:40 but 25:41, "Out of my sight, you condemned, and into that everlasting fire prepared for the devil and his angels."

Act, Maureen. The time is now.

Action, on all fronts. She came out of her depression. She cleaned house, cooked for the children, was the companion and lover of Dr. Alan Harrison, worked hard with the board of education.

At home alone, when the kids were in school, she checked out the garage to be sure the ingredients were on hand. They were—a rickety pail, a rubber siphon, a flat box that contained the packets of matches Josh used to light his Bunsen burner, dirty rags. The siphon was an heirloom; it had come down to them from Jack Mercer's time. It was a narrow rubber tube, like a catheter, and its purpose was to siphon out gasoline, when necessary, from the gas tank of an automobile. All necessaries present and accounted for.

Today was the day. Friday, March twelfth. It was bitter cold, the skies were sullen; Maureen wondered whether it would snow. She shook her head. Snow in March? In nine days it would be spring. Laurie was spending the weekend with the Harrisons. Josh would be home for a weekend of chemistry experiments. She would go to Jackson City to repair the transmission. It was vital that this weekend the car be in perfect working order.

She picked up the kids from school, deposited Laurie at the Harrison house, took off for home with Josh. On the way the car acted up.

"You did say," Josh said, "that you called that Rick Perry and told him you were coming."

"I did, this morning."

"It's a long drive to Jackson City, forty-five miles."

"I'll be on my way the minute I drop you off at the house."

"I hope you make it—"

"I'll make it."

Very little was said the rest of the way home.

It was a long, boring drive to Jackson City. Rick Perry turned out to be a brawny, open-faced young man, optimistic but not very happy about her car. "After you called me," he said, "I called your mechanic Tom Duffy in Acheron, and he said all you need is a coupla parts. Well, you need them coupla parts, but your boat needs a helluva lot more fixin' up before she's ready to roll all clear. I know you come in to me on a forty-five-mile drive, and I can do up the job a hunnerd percent, but I'm gonna need four-five hours, which I'm willin' to do, seein' you come in all the way for Rick Perry. So I tell you what, Miz Blair. You go see yerself a movie and maybe have yerself a nice dinner here in town. Gimme me four-five hours—maybe less—and I will give you back your Ford station wagon which I guarantee will run the roads for the next two-three years minimum. It is gonna cost you, Miz Blair, but I guarantee . . ."

When she came back to Rick Perry it was early evening and, damn it, it was beginning to snow. "I give it the full attention, Miz Blair, and I guarantee you she'll run real good for the next two-three years."

He presented his bill and she found it to be, for all his time and work, quite reasonable. She did offer him extra

208

money but he laughed it off. "That extra money," he said in a solemn voice but in bright-eyed wry Maine humor, "has already been figgered into the bill. Now how's about some gas and oil?"

"Yes," she said. "Please fill the tank, and whatever oil is necessary."

He did the gas and oil, she paid him.

"Looks like we're comin' up with like a real snowstorm," he said. "If you wanna stay over here in town like till mornin' I got places I can recommend."

"I'd rather not. It's only forty-five miles."

"Well, you got good snow tires, and now you got a sound car. It'll be slow goin' but if you got the nerve I don't figger you'll have no problems."

It was a long slow ride home, the snow blowing southwesterly. She had set the coming day for the work that had to be done, but there were moments—the chugging windshield wipers giving off poor vision—when she wondered whether she should not have postponed, whether she should not have stayed over in Jackson City, whether she would not get bogged down somewhere on a strange road, the car immobilized and she, inside it, trapped in falling snow. Trapped, freezing, suffocating. *No*, damn it. . . .

She made it without incident, but it was four in the morning when she arrived at the house. The snow was ending, the storm was over. She parked the car in the road away from the house, which had been part of her original plan. She would have said—and there would have been no one to deny her—that the garage door was stuck and therefore she had left the car outside. Now she had a better reason; the snow, piled up against the garage door, had made it immovable . . .

Actually there was very little snow at the garage door; the brisk-blowing southwest winds had kept that part of the house, the northwest, virtually clear, and also the front of the house. The great drifts, piled high, were at the other end; there were hills of snow, blotting out the exterior of the recreation room, and rising almost to Laurie's bedroom.

Maureen, keys in hand, ran into the house and upstairs to her bedroom. She put on the small bed lamp, stripped out of her clothes. She put on her warmest, thickest, woolliest pajamas, put a bathrobe on a chair near the bed, and arranged her wool-lined bedroom slippers on the floor near the chair. She took off her wristwatch, put it on the bed table, got into bed. She turned to the clock on the bed table, set the alarm for six o'clock. She switched off the bed lamp and lay on her back under the covers, eyes closed. She did not sleep. She lay on her back in the darkness, her eyes closed, forced her mind to be blank. But she did not sleep. She could not sleep.

When the alarm rang she grabbed at the clock, switched it off. The preliminaries of dawn were like small candles behind the veil of the sky, but that vague light was enough for her. She got into the bathrobe and slid into the wool-lined bedroom slippers. She reached toward her wristwatch, but her hand snapped back from it. You don't take time to put on a wristwatch when you're supposedly running from a burning house. A nearby bathrobe and slippers, yes. Almost instinctive, the quick need to cover the body for warmth, protection . . . but a wristwatch no.

She went out into the corridor and walked northward, to Josh's room. Outside his door she stepped out of her slippers, turned the knob, and on bare feet entered the large bedroom. Josh, notoriously a heavy sleeper, was lying on his stomach, spread-eagled, snoring. She crossed to the north window, and from the nail in that wall took off the key that could open the accordian gate that was strung across that window. Next she removed the key from the west window. She returned to the half-open thick oak door, extracted the big iron key from the lock, went out, pulled the door closed, inserted the key, turned the lock and withdrew the key.

Whoever he was in there—he was securely locked inside that room. No way he could break out.

She stepped back into her bedroom slippers, and with three keys clinking in a pocket of her bathrobe, she went down the stairs and out into the cold morning, the first pale streaks of dawn disclosing a white landscape of softening snow. She did not use the gizmo. She lifted the garage door halfway up. Stooping, she entered the garage. She took the keys from the pocket of her bathrobe and dropped them to the floor of the garage. She found the rickety old pail and the old rubber siphon. She coiled the siphon and dropped it into the pail, hooked her fingers to the handle of the pail and went out with it to the car.

She twisted off the cap of the gas tank and placed the pail on the ground directly beneath that side of the tank. Squatting, she inserted one end of the siphon into the gas tank and put the other end into her mouth. She sucked until the gasoline came. The taste was awful. She spat it out, dropped that end of the siphon into the pail and the gasoline flowed. When the pail was half-full she withdrew the siphon and replaced the cap of the tank.

Carrying siphon and pail she trudged back, stooped under the door and reentered the garage. She tossed away the rubber siphon. She set the pail down and looked about. The back wall would do it. Once ignited, the back wall would carry the fire up into the bedroom. And then the whole house would go. It had no resistance to fire. Steve had installed a few hand-propelled fire extinguishers, good for extinguishing any small sudden fire. But a real fire, an accelerated fire, would doom the whole house; it was all wood, and old dried-out wood. It was virtually a tall tinderbox.

She took up a rag and a packet of matches. She took up the pail, tossed its contents against the rear wall, dropped the pail. She moved back. She struck a match to the rag and threw it to the rear wall, which immediately became a wall of fire. She turned and ran out of the garage, and for

211

whatever the reason—there was no thought-out reason—
she slammed down the garage door and ran to the car and
stood leaning against it, and saw the orange flames in the
windows of the bedroom above the garage.

And then she heard the noise.

She would never forget it but would never be able to
describe it. It reached into her soul, left its mark. It reached
upward to a fearsome crescendo—and stopped.

Blessed relief. But only for a moment. Because now there
was another noise . . . a scream that came from the other
end of the house, the south end. The north end was briskly
burning and would soon collapse. The middle, at the entrance,
was still negotiable; and the south end, although smoky,
was still clear of the encroaching fire. Maureen ran to her
right, toward the sound of the screaming; she ran to the
south end of the house and looked up over the hill of snow
that covered the recreation room. She looked up to Laurie's
bedroom.

And saw Laurie.

She was standing at the open window, screaming, her
face blurred by the crisscross of the iron accordian gate.

Why was she there?

Why was Laurie in the house?

And now it was Maureen whose voice rode a crescendo.
"Open up that gate. Open the gate and jump. Laurie, do
you hear me? *Open up that gate.*"

But the child just stood there at the window, no longer
screaming. She had seen her mother, and now in her hysteria
was no longer making a sound. Maureen took in the situation.
For whatever reason the child was in the house, she had
awakened to smoke and fire. She had run to the door, retreat
was blocked by fire. In panic she had thrust her hands
through the accordian gate and raised the window, but she'd
been so long accustomed to the gate that in her panic she
believed it to be a permanence. Panic induced paralysis. All

the child could do was stand there at an open window and silently scream through the crisscross bars of an iron gate. Maureen's words did not penetrate. The child just stood there . . .

Maureen ran into the burning house, all smoke and heat and fire and grime, and up the stairs already aflame, and as she got to the top and turned to the right, toward Laurie's room, the burning stairs collapsed behind her.

She ran into the bedroom.

"*Laurie.*"

The child did not turn. She stood staring out the window through the latticework of the iron gate. She was barefoot. She was wearing long-legged wool pajamas.

Maureen plucked the key from the nail on the wall and opened the gate. "*Jump,*" she said. "There's snow out there, a big hill of snow. We can't get hurt."

But the child, frozen in hysteria, just stood there. Maureen seized hold of a shoulder and whirled her around. Her eyes, her big blue eyes, staring, were utterly vacant. Maureen hit her, slapped her across the face, and did it again and again until, abruptly, the blue eyes were seeing, and even better, showed fear.

Red-orange flames were now licking at the doorway. Unless they did something quickly, unless they moved now, they would die.

Maureen pointed at the open window.

Laurie looked at her, hesitated, then seemed to take hold of herself, ran and jumped out.

Maureen quickly followed.

They helped each other, sloshing out of the high snowdrift. They went to the car, near the heat of the burning house but far enough away for safety. Without a word Maureen opened the door on the passenger's side and Laurie slid in. Maureen went round to the rear of the station wagon and found two dirty old blankets. She returned to the other

213

side, the driver's side, and clambered in, losing one of her bedroom slippers as she did. Laurie wrapped herself in one of the blankets, and her bare feet in the other.

"All right?" Maureen finally said. These were the first words between them since they'd jumped.

"Yes . . ."

"Laurie . . . what in God's name were you doing here? You were supposed to be spending the weekend with Diana. You were supposed to be sleeping over, the weekend . . ."

"The snowstorm," Laurie said.

Her voice was flat, as though she were still partly in shock . . . not yet fully aware (which was a good thing, Maureen decided). The child needed time before coming fully awake, before realizing what must have happened to her brother. Time . . . they both needed it. "Go on, honey."

"It came over on the TV . . . there was going to be a snowstorm. Dr. Harrison . . . he was finished in the office, it was dark . . . I asked him to please drive me home, the weatherman said it might be a big one and I didn't want to be stuck away from you and Josh so he did that, drove me home and went back. He wanted to be with Diana. Josh said you were stuck in Jackson City fixing the car, you'd be home late . . ." Her voice fell off, she seemed to be nodding off.

"Dr. Harrison drove right back? He didn't know I wasn't home. Didn't he come in for a moment to say hello?"

". . . Oh, yes . . . that's right, he did. Josh told him what he told me, told both of us at the same time. I promised I'd call him as soon as we heard from you. Snow was already beginning to fall, he could have got caught in the storm . . ."

"You did right, honey, and so did he." Keep talking, she told herself, put off a bit longer the girl's inevitable confrontation, the shock of it . . . "Anything else, Laurie? I mean, when I didn't come home did you maybe call Dr. Harrison?"

"Yes . . . I did, but I didn't get through to him. The operator said the lines were down in Acheron Falls."

214

"Happens every snowstorm."

"Then Josh and I ate some supper and I tried to call again but this time nothing, our phone was dead."

"Which meant all the lines were down. I couldn't call."

"That's what Josh said, and he said what with all this snow you'd probably be staying over in Jackson City."

Maureen struggled to keep the child talking. Behind them the burning house was too far off to be a danger to them, but it was near enough for its heat to hold them comfortable in the car. Talk was supposed to be therapy, a relief from hysteria. But she knew that as the hysteria dissipated the question would come . . . "You know me, Laurie, I'm stubborn. It wasn't really a blizzard. It was a snowstorm like lots of others up here in Maine. From Jackson City to Acheron Falls its mostly state highway and the state people are very good, they get those trucks out fast to shovel off the snow and salt and sand the roadbeds. I'm not saying it was exactly a picnic but I did all right, thanks to my brand-new snow tires. Slow going, though. I got home, it must have been four o'clock. Only the roads near home were real bad . . ." She saw the question beginning to form in the child's eyes. She kept talking. "What time did you kids go to sleep?"

"What? Oh . . . about eleven, I guess. I wrote a note for you, saying I was home and how Dr. Harrison drove me home. I attached it to the fridge like we always do and then went up to sleep . . ."

"Never saw your note," Maureen said. "Never got to the kitchen. Got into the house and switched lights on and off, quicklike, running up to my bedroom . . ."

The question in Laurie's eyes was formed, and momentarily, it would be expressed. Maureen channeled her talk, quick-time, to the inevitable . . . "It must have been about six o'clock when I woke up. I don't know what woke me but it must have been the sound of the fire, the crackling sound of fire and the smoke. I grabbed my bathrobe and slippers, ran out into the hall. God, Laurie, the north end of the house was inferno, I couldn't get past it, I just ran

215

down the stairs and out . . . The car was parked here because when I got home the garage door was socked in with snow and the remote-control gizmo didn't work . . . I kept hitting that button but the door didn't move. The north end of the house was burning like mad but I stayed out here by the car hoping against hope . . . and then, honey, then I heard the screaming from your end of the house, from your bedroom. I ran there and at the window I saw you—"

"Must have been what woke me too," Laurie picked it up. "The fire, the smoke . . . I got out of bed and ran to the door and the smoke hit me and I could see fire out there . . . I shut the door, ran to the window and shoved my hands through the wide-open slots of the gate and pulled up the window but somehow I forgot the gate was a gate, somehow it was a part of the house . . . I was crazy, I know it . . . I mean waking up from sleep and opening the door and there's that awful fire out there . . . something went in my mind and I just stood there by the open window, screaming, like crazy . . . Oh, *mom* . . . tell me, what about . . . ?"

Maureen leaned over and gathered the child in her arms and held her close. And then, at last, she came out with it."

"Josh?" Laurie said. "What about *Josh* . . . ?"

Maureen held her, kissed her cheeks, her chin, her forehead.

"Mom, tell me . . . Oh, God, please tell me he's okay . . . ?"

Maureen kept stroking her hair, took a deep breath. "Darling, Josh is gone—"

"*No* . . . *no* . . . Oh God, please no. How? Why couldn't he get out . . . *mom* . . ."

"Darling, I'm afraid Josh started the fire. Of course not meaning to . . . His chemistry experiments, he must have been really keen on this one . . . he must have gotten up early in the morning to work on it . . . Remember I told you about Alan telling him a Bunsen burner could be a fire hazard. Josh didn't worry, but I guess this morning it was

216

so early . . . he was sleepy and he must have gotten care-less . . ."

And now, finally, the child was crying, shaking, letting it out. Maureen reached across to the glove compartment, took out some tissues . . . more than anything as a distraction . . . and Laurie pressed them to her eyes—

There was a roar, a tremendous roar that broke them apart, forced them to turn their heads to see what had happened behind them.

The house had collapsed. The burning house had fallen in on itself. It was a high, smoldering heap, burning sluggishly, like a funeral pyre.

And now Maureen was weeping too, merging her own suppressed feelings, so different than Laura's, with the girl's outpouring of shock and grief. She took Laura's face in her hands, kissed her, tried to comfort them both . . . From the east the risen sun laid a patina of light across the sodden sky. Morning had come, but a dull, gray wintry morning; a morning that aptly merged with the horrific events of the darkness only a short time before.

Gently, Maureen separated herself from her daughter, still wrapped within the rough blanket so that only her face peaked out. She reached down to the ignition key and was about to turn it when, wordlessly, Laura pointed downward. At first confused, Maureen followed her daughter's gesture and saw that her right foot was unshod, that somewhere between the house and the car she'd dropped a slipper. A detail, a sane concrete detail for both of them to reach for and cling to in the midst of this tragedy that neither could give full expression to . . . at least not yet.

Maureen looked at her daughter, stroked her head and managed a half smile. "That's your mother, darling. Half here and half there." She looked to her left out the window, and surprisingly, there it was, lying in the snow. "Be right back," she said, suddenly feeling it was of huge importance that she retrieve the slipper, at least make *something* whole again, bring some little symmetry to her life, even if it were so minuscule a matter as this. She stepped out onto the snowy ground, slid her right foot into the errant slipper— and the pain struck.

Up from her womb and down from the base of her abdomen. A stabbing, searing pain. Her groin was on fire, trapped in a spasm that threw her forward across the hood of the car. She knew what was happening, and prayed it would continue to happen. And it did. Somewhere a passageway seemed to open inside her, she felt a warm viscous flow, out of her and down her thighs, and she unashamedly thanked God . . .

She lay across the hood of the car for several moments, letting the pain ebb, trying to compose herself before facing Laurie again. Finally she stood up, breathing deeply, retied the belt of her robe and got back into the car. In answer to Laurie's inquiring look, she put her arm around the girl, and pulled her close, needing the warmth of her daughter as much as her daughter needed her.

"I love you, Laurie," she said. Remember that, no matter what. A benediction, an injunction, a commitment.

The child huddled down and even closer to her mother as Maureen turned on the ignition, switched on the heater and commenced the slow journey over snow-clogged roads toward the township of Acheron Falls, and the home of Alan Harrison, where her life, and her daughter's, would have a safe haven in which to begin once again. . . .